THE LAST ONES

T. MICHELLE NELSON

The characters and events depicted in this book are fictitious. Any similarities to actual events or persons, living or dead, are coincidental and not intended by the author.

The Last Ones
Copyright © 2016 T. Michelle Nelson
All rights reserved.

Cover Art by Najla Qamber
Back Cover Photos by Toni A. Wolf
Back Cover Makeup Artist and Model: Chris Pezzano

DEDICATION:

THIS BOOK IS DEDICATED TO BRIAN, WHO HELPED
INSPIRE IT, BUT WON'T READ IT.

PROLOGUE

Sheena was an undeniably beautiful girl. She was an art major and had true a skill in painting. She'd even turned her face into a work of art. Sheena's eyeliner was done like a pin-up girl's from the forties and it made her baby blues really pop. They weren't really blue anymore though. They were more of a cloudy white as they stared back up at Evie. They were still pretty. Pretty and unblinking.

Evie knew she should try calling the police, but wasn't sure how she would explain what had happened, even if she could reach the authorities. She ran through the events of the morning and the night before. Every action, every word the two girls had spoken replayed in her mind. Somehow she would make sense of it all. Evie needed to reconcile all that had taken place and understand how she had managed to kill her own best friend.

CHAPTER ONE

The door creaked open quietly. Sheena was always coming in late. She tiptoed in a half-hearted effort to feign respect of Evie's sleep schedule each time, and each time she woke her roommate. Evie went to bed promptly by midnight after long hours at the hospital each day. Sometimes she even went to bed earlier. Sheena, on the other hand, stayed out late, partied and mingled at exhibits until the wee hours. They were both planning for their futures in their chosen fields, but in very different ways.

Evie rose each morning before the sun in order to be prompt and fully awake when she arrived at the hospital. She would someday have her own practice, and her ambition to become a respected and knowledgeable physician was rivaled only by Sheena's ambition to meet that one gallery owner or rich benefactor who would help her become the art world's new big thing.

The events Sheena attended often ran very late and encouraged celebration with a variety of spirits. Once again, she was coming in a bit inebriated as she stumbled through the door and crashed into the accent table where Evie always kept her phone, keys and hospital identification.

"Drunk again?" Evie shouted from her bedroom. This wasn't the first time Sheena had come home and knocked the furniture around. Evie had recognized the banging sound of the table bumping the wall and it's contents being jostled.

"Little bit, but I could use some of that expertise of yours, Doc," Sheena slurred.

Evie drug herself from the twin bed, shook her head a bit and rubbed her eyes. Stumbling, as though she were drunk herself, she wandered into the living room of their ultra-affordable, and tiny apartment. Dressed in a very short, fire engine red cocktail dress and ridiculously tall stilettos Sheena wobbled with a bloody Kleenex pressed to her arm.

"Do you need stitches? What did you do?" Evie asked.

"I didn't fall this time. Some jackass bit me!" Sheena exclaimed.

Puzzled by the statement, Evie held Sheena's wrist and removed the makeshift compress. Sure enough, a superficial bite mark was exposed.

"Why did someone bite you?" Evie asked.

"I have no idea. I was too drunk to drive, so I took a cab from the gallery. We cut through campus and all these fraternity boys rushed the cab. It's not even football season, but they were in full riot mode! I had my window rolled down because I felt a little sick and one of them grabbed my arm through the window and bit me! The cab driver sped off because they were surrounding the car, but I didn't even get a really good look at him. I want to report the douchebag for assault, but I'll probably never find out who he is!"

"We should go to the hospital. You could get something from this," Evie explained, hoping she wasn't scaring her roommate.

"Like what? Rabies?" Sheena laughed.

"I'm serious, like hepatitis, even herpes. You need a tetanus shot anyway," Evie's tone grew serious.

"He just bit me, Evie. I didn't sleep with him! Herpes? Are you serious?"

"Dead serious. Let me throw on some clothes and we'll go now. Go wash the wound out with soap and water and put some of that cream I have in the medicine cabinet in the yellow and brown tube on it afterwards," Evie instructed.

As Evie pulled on her pants loud screams and gunshots resounded from outside her bedroom, startling the pre-med student. She fell over with her jeans around her knees.

"Sheena! Is that the TV?" Evie yelled. It was just like her roommate to ignore her instructions and watch some stupid late-night horror movie instead of doing what needed to be done.

"Evie, it's outside the apartment," Sheena whispered from the door. "People are running around crazy and shooting!"

Evie flung the door open to find her roommate wide-eyed and serious.

"They're shooting?" Evie questioned.

Sheena nodded her head.

"They've set things on fire before, but this is insane!" Evie exclaimed.

"This bite isn't going to kill me. There's no way we can go out in that!" Sheena cried.

"Call 9-1-1 and tell them what's happening. I'm going to call my attending at the hospital and ask if he knows what's going on."

Neither of the calls went through any number of times the girls attempted. Evie rested her head against Sheena's shoulder on the couch and sighed. She wouldn't risk taking her half-drunk roommate through college rioting. The noises from outside were getting louder and closer.

"Let's turn off the lights. I don't think we should draw attention to ourselves from the street," Sheena advised.

"Good idea," Evie agreed.

As Sheena pulled the heavy curtains over the blinds and flipped the light switches, Evie turned on the television and quickly lowered the volume. Scenes from all over Columbus, Ohio flashed across the screen. The suburbs of Hilliard, Grove City, Powell, and Reynoldsburg all reported disturbances and newscasters offered no explanation. An aerial view of downtown from the Channel 6TV chopper showed hundreds of people running down the streets and attacking others.

"What is happening!" Evie bellowed.

"Maybe it's a zombie apocalypse," Sheena stated in a somber tone.

"Be serious. What are we supposed to do while all this rioting is going on? We can't get through to any emergency services on the phone and we're trapped."

"Let's just chill out. This can't last for long before the cops get a handle on it, right?" Sheena reasoned.

"What if someone tries to break in here?" Evie asked.

Sheena loudly sighed and slapped her hands down on the cushions of the couch as she raised herself up and exited the room. Momentarily, she returned.

"We'll use this," Sheena waved a handgun around her head with little regard to gun safety.

"When did you get *that*?" Evie shouted and rushed to take the gun from her roommate's hands. As Evie examined the gun she became irritated to find it was loaded with a full clip.

"My brother gave it to me when we moved in here. He said living in town like this was dangerous for two girls alone," Sheena rolled her eyes as she repeated her sibling's words.

"What's dangerous is you having a gun and not knowing how to use it. You could've shot me just now waving it around your head like that!"

"I'm sorry. You keep it, but have it handy tonight. Who knows what could happen."

***

The girls turned the volume on the television down to a quiet whisper. They could still hear the unnerving noises of screaming, banging and occasional shooting coming from the street, but they also listened to the news reports that were steadily coming in from all the local channels.

More aerial shots of the hordes of angry people were shown, and a few of the reporters were filming live from the quieter streets or rooftops. As ridiculous as the thought was, many of the people who were broadcast repeated Sheena's sentiments, that the masses of looters were not people at all, but instead zombies.

"Hey, every time someone says zombie, we should do a shot!" Sheena suggested.

"The entire city is under attack and you want to get drunker than you already are?" Evie questioned.

"I'm just nervous. This is insane!" Sheena attempted to justify her illogical proposition.

"Okay, one shot if someone else says zombie, just to knock the edge off. Deal?" Evie agreed.

"I'll get the tequila!" Sheena shouted, a bit too loud and raced into their kitchen returning with a bottle.

"Here with us is Ohio State physician and professor, Dr. Thomas Stillman, who has been working at the medical center all evening treating the victims of these horrific riots."

"Oh my gosh, turn it up, that's one of my professors!" Evie exclaimed.

"As implausible as this may seem, the victims of these attacks still have motor function after clinical death. The only explanation I can offer at this time is that corpses of the recently deceased are reanimating and attacking the living," Dr. Stillman's face continued to appear solemn with no promise of a later 'just kidding.'

"Excuse me, Dr. Stillman? Can you elaborate?" The newslady asked.

"Zombies. They're zombies, woman!" Dr. Stillman addressed the camera and began to speak directly to the viewers. *"If you are near someone who has recently passed, be prepared to get away quickly. Stay away from hospitals and crowded areas. If you have been bitten..."*

The camera quickly returned to an anchorman sitting behind the desk safely in the station. The bewildered look on his face would have been great fodder any other time, but instead of laughing, Evie and Sheena waited in anticipation for him to say something. Anything.

"Looks like April Fool's Day came early this year!" the anchorman finally chortled and laughed uncomfortably.

"That guy was your teacher? He's a doctor?" Sheena asked.

"Yes," Evie answered.

"Does he joke much?"

"No."

"What do you think he was going to say about being bitten?" Sheena questioned.

"I'm not sure," Evie answered.

"You're a doctor! You knew I could get herpes or hepatitis, what was he going to say? What is going to happen to me?" Sheena demanded.

"Nothing, I'm sure. This is all ridiculous! There are no zombies. I don't know why he would go on television and say something like that. He's mean and disgruntled and maybe it was his attempt at a joke. Maybe he believes it, but I'm telling you, once something is dead, it doesn't come back and try to eat people. There are no such things," Evie reassured.

"If it's calm in the morning, can I go into the hospital with you?" Sheena began to cry.

"Of course, honey. Just calm down," Evie wrapped her arm around Sheena and rubbed her shoulders. "This will all be fine. Some idiot just bit you, you aren't going to die."

A loud smashing sound made both girl's jump, and Evie without thinking, immediately reached for her roommate's gun, which rested at her side. The source of the disturbance was revealed a moment later. Relieved to find it was only Floyd, their housecat, who had knocked a salt shaker off the counter, both girls audibly sighed.

"I have to be at the hospital in a few hours. Let's try to get some sleep," Evie offered.

"Can I sleep with you?" Sheena asked.

"We can both sleep in here. It will probably be best if we stayed close and by the gun," Evie reasoned.

Sheena threw herself on the couch, rubbed her eyes, and lightly ran her finger across the bite mark on her forearm. Evie noticed a single tear run down her roommate's cheek.

"Hey, everything is going to be okay," Evie warmly reassured.

"This is some scary crap, Ev."

"Think about that fantastic portrait you did of me and how soon someone is going to see what an amazing artist you are and your work is going to sell for millions."

"Artwork doesn't sell for millions until the artist is dead," Sheena mumbled.

"Oh, stop it. You aren't going to die. Once this place is calmed down I'll help you hunt down that little freak that bit you and we will tune him up," Evie wagged her eyebrows as she motioned like she was punching an invisible person.

"Tune him up? Who are you?" Sheena laughed.

"Sorry, I knew some rough customers back home. Sometimes some of that lingo sticks with you!"

Evie threw a blanket on the floor across the room from the couch where Sheena sat. She curled up in the fetal position and watched her friend do the same on their hand-me-down plaid sofa. Evie shut her eyes with a smile on her face. The entire town might be falling down around them, Evie thought, but at least she had calmed her roommate and she felt good about herself. That was a huge perk in going into medicine. When she could help someone, it made her feel like a superhero.

Before she drifted off into a dreamless sleep, the last thing Evie saw was Floyd. The ill-behaved stray cat had jumped atop Sheena and began pulling at the covers with his claws and finally nestled in the bend of the girl's legs. Sheena reached down and petted the animal she had begged Evie to take in some months before.

***

Evie sighed. The alarm on her phone hadn't gone off yet, making her all too aware that she had barely gotten only a few hours sleep, yet she was awake. She reluctantly opened her eyes and wiped them with her fingers as she sat up. Something had startled her to consciousness, but she had no idea what. The room was dark, and Evie's eyes hadn't adjusted but she felt around on the floor until she recognized the shape and feel of her roommate's handgun.

A crunching noise, followed by squishing sounds drew her attention toward the couch and where her roommate had fallen asleep. The wet, mushy, smacking noises subsided for only a moment before they began again. Evie slowly rose and carefully tiptoed to the nearest lamp, feeling for the button. With a click, the room filled with light. Only feet away crouched on the couch was her roommate, Sheena, her face buried in Floyd's fur. The cat made no noise but Sheena's sloppy smacking continued as she buried her face deeper into the fur. It was clear to Evie what used to be Floyd was now only a lifeless rag of fur and blood. Sheena immediately raised her gaze from the feline carcass to Evie, yet still face deep in the midsection of the animal, entrails spilling from her mouth as she continued to chew.

"Sheena! What the heck?" Evie screamed.

Sheena's eyes widened and the dead cat fell to the floor. Her head cocked uncomfortably to one side and she opened her mouth, but instead of an explanation, the only thing to escape was a deep moan.

Within seconds, Sheena was pushing through their second hand furniture, scrambling with arms outreached and flailing to reach Evie. Sheena fell over the coffee table that she and Evie had repainted together when they moved into the apartment, breaking the wobbly leg that had never been fixed. Her moans became loud growls and Sheena quickly clambered back to her feet to rush toward Evie once again.

"Sheena, please stop!" Evie cried.

The words were of no avail, Sheena not only didn't respond to Evie's pleading, she no longer seemed to even comprehend.

Just as Sheena's outstretched arm reached her roommate, Evie screamed, raised the handgun and pulled the trigger. Sheena stilled and fell to the floor with a thud.

Moments later Evie collapsed. Her muscles each like gelatin, felt useless and weak. Evie stared wide-eyed at the corpse on the floor. Her lungs burned just as her ears did from the shot and she gasped for breath.

What had just happened? She repeatedly asked herself. She had just shot her roommate in the head.

CHAPTER TWO

Hours passed, Evie knew it must have been a quite some time because daylight had begun to peak through the drapes. Once the shock began wearing off, Evie covered Sheena's body with a blanket. She repeated the process because she could hardly stand to look at poor Floyd, the cat, much more than the cadaver of her roommate. No, Sheena wasn't a cadaver like in Anatomy Lab. She was a victim. Of what, Evie questioned. Sure, Evie had pulled the trigger and ended Sheena's life, but she needed to believe and understand something else had caused the chain of events that brought her to that unforgivable act.

Sheena had hastened toward Evie in a threatening way, like a menacing animal. She hadn't spoken, only growled. She had eaten their pet cat. To be sure, Evie decided to examine the feline. *Could it have been possible that Sheena had been playing a horrible joke on her and she had accidently killed her friend for it?*

To Evie's confusion, the carcass Sheena had been munching on was in fact, Floyd. His matted, bloodied fur was quite real and beyond disgusting. Evie gagged, and swallowed hard, pushing back the urge to vomit. Medical school required a strong stomach, but she'd seen nothing like this. It made no sense. Zombies weren't real. That couldn't be an explanation.

Once the cat was covered again, Evie began to analyze the situation. She had no idea what to do. If she called the police and explained what had happened, would she be arrested and convicted of murdering her roommate? Was what she had done in fact an act of self defense? Even she wasn't sure. Regardless, she had to do something.

Reluctantly, Evie picked up the phone and dialed 9-1-1. Her hands shook as she punched in the numbers. Shaking, she held the phone to her ear only to hear the rapid succession of a busy dial tone, then a recording that stated the number could not be completed as dialed.

Evie screamed. What began as a cry of desperation, grew louder and louder until Evie lost her voice and silently sobbed. Sheena was the only person she was close to in the city. Her other friends had moved on to different internships and the students who had remained to complete training with Evie were little more than acquaintances. She had no one nearby to contact. How she would contact someone, even if there were help, she had no idea with no phone service.

Dropping the phone to her side, Evie staggered to the front door. The blood on her hands, most likely from Floyd since she hadn't touched Sheena's corpse very much, made the knob slippery and difficult to turn. When she finally managed to pull it open, sunlight blinded her.

Evie blinked hard repeatedly until she could clearly see the scene outside her apartment. Her mouth fell open, and she crumbled to the ground as the grisly sights came into focus. The maintenance man, a hulking, yet attractive Mexican fellow named Antonio crouched over the body of old Mrs. Barnes, the sweet widow lady who made cookies for the children who played in the parking lot of the apartment complex. Mrs. Barnes' intestines were pulled from her body and stretched to Antonio's mouth. He slurped up small sections at a time like large strands of spaghetti.

By the office building, Rosyln, the beautiful brunette secretary who always answered the phones and took care of any complaints stood amidst the courtyard naked and bloodied. She was obviously in shock, stumbling without her clothes, staring at the ground before her. Evie rose to her feet, wobbly at first, but with purpose as she sprinted to help the poor secretary.

"Roz!" Evie shouted in a loud whisper in her haste to reach the woman.

Roslyn quickly turned to face Evie in an inhuman, animalistic motion. Half of her jaw was missing, and she sported only the hole of her eye socket with no meat or eyeball left. Evie skidded to a stop, almost falling. Too terrified to even scream Evie watched Roslyn hunker her shoulders, cock her head to the side and distend it forward as her neck twisted, like a rabid dog about to attack. The last warning before the secretary began to rush her was an abysmal growl that seemed to emanate deep from within her throat.

Evie spun in the direction she had come pushing her legs to the ground with force, her feet digging in with each step in an attempt to run as hard and fast as she could toward the still open door of her apartment.

The few yards seemed as though they were miles as Evie hurtled toward the door, and though she dared not look back, she was certain the grunting and heavy footfalls behind her inched closer with each step. Once across the threshold, Evie slammed and immediately bolted the door.

She stood in silence for a few moments, wondering if she should peek out the window, but just as the thought ran through her head a loud thud startled it away. Grunting, growling and scratching at the door Roslyn persisted in her efforts reach Evie. It was more than an hour before the noises subsided and all became quiet again.

Evie, with her knees pulled up to her chest, sat quietly cowering in her kitchen behind the small island attempting to rationally explain what was happening in her world. Sure, it could be some infectious disease, maybe even a biological weapon that had been used somehow, but regardless of the cause, there were a few things she now knew. The incubation period on a living person was a matter of a few short hours. Symptoms of infected patients were like a Rottweiler on PCP and the prognosis was... zombies. The things outside that were once people were clearly no longer human. They didn't seem to feel pain or have any rational thought. They were aggressive and their focus seemed to be on attacking other living creatures that were not infected.

Evie took a deep breath, nodded her head in agreement with her diagnosis, as crazy as it sounded, and decided to make a plan. Her family was almost four hundred miles away. Was this a global pandemic? Were they safe? Even if her rural hometown in Kentucky was affected it would still be safer than being in the fifteenth largest city in the United States. Not to mention she just wanted to be with her loved ones and make sure they were okay.

Evie's ten-year-old Ford Escape ran like a dream, but trekking four hundred miles seemed impossible even in a reliable vehicle. She had no idea what she would run into along the way and she would have to go through two other large cities – Cincinnati and Louisville. Driving was risky and she knew it, but there was possibly another option.

Evie weighed the idea. She had the know-how, she had her license, but she did not have a plane. Since she began her undergraduate studies, Evie had been a member of the OSU Flying Club. They had several different planes, one of which was the same model she had learned to fly on, an identical one to the plane her Uncle Delmont had taken her up in since she was a child, a four-seater Mooney, single engine. It was a wonderful little aircraft. Many people found them temperamental, but not Evie. She was most comfortable flying it.

The airfield was roughly ten miles from her apartment through town. If no one had opened the fence that morning, it would be secure and she could somehow maybe break in, get the keys to the Mooney and stay a few thousand feet above any threats on the ground all the way home. Evie rationalized it was the best option for her, but only if she actually could make it up in the air. What if the runway was overrun with these afflicted persons? What if she couldn't find a key?

Uncle Delmont had once told her with a hammer and a small screwdriver, you could start a Mooney without the key, but would it work? She wasn't exactly MacGyver. No matter, her options were becoming quite limited and she had to act soon. The noises outside were getting louder and the only barrier between her and the chaos was several plates of glass in each of the windows in her apartment.

Evie's hands shook as she attempted to logically think of anything she might need. In a large duffel, she packed some snacks, water, all the kitchen knives she owned as well as a few changes of comfortable clothes. As she steeled her nerves and began toward the front door, she grabbed her keys and her OSU Flying Club membership card. Evie laughed to herself. She wasn't sure why she had grabbed the card, since her intentions weren't to exactly check out the plane and return it. She would be stealing it.

Evie hung the duffel over her shoulder, held her keys in one hand, her dead roommate's handgun in the other. She stared at her front door for several moments psyching herself up for the mad dash she was about to make to her car.

"One, two, two-and-a-half, two-and-three-quarters..." Evie counted, and finally grabbed the doorknob, gave it a hard fast turn and quickly scanned the area.

Two zombies she didn't recognize lumbered by the office building where Roslyn had been earlier. Old Mrs. Barnes body was little but a head, arms and part of a torso with a string of messy flesh and disgorged tissue from her chest hanging behind. Her arms twitched and her head turned from side to side. She was obviously not a threat in the condition she was in, however, it was difficult for Evie to pull her eyes away from the squirming remains of her elderly neighbor.

A stray dog barked, grabbing her attention to the right toward the parking lot and Evie's only mode of transportation. A horde of zombies chased after it causing Evie to freeze in place and hope none of the once again living corpses spotted her.

When all seemed quiet, Evie cautiously advanced toward her car, staying close to the building and keeping a watch of her surroundings. Once at the edge of the apartment complex, Evie readjusted the strap on her duffel, making sure it was fashioned tightly on her shoulder, she positioned her thumb on the keychain button to unlock her car door and griped the handgun firmly with her finger on the trigger.

Instead of pausing to count to three and fortify her courage, Evie took off across the small expanse of parking lot like Carl Lewis. She pumped her arms, running hard and fast without looking back and hurdled over debris, which consisted mostly of body parts, littering her path. With a few feet to go, Evie double-clicked the unlock button on the Ford, audibly heard the locks release and without slowing slammed into the driver's side door.

Hastily, Evie shoved her duffel in the passenger seat, jumped in and started the ignition. Although her Ford had never had any problems, it always seemed to take a few seconds to turn over. The seconds drug on like days as she waited before she threw the vehicle in reverse and stomped on the gas.

A 'thump' from the rear of her car alarmed Evie, however, she didn't stop or even slow as she swatted the gear shifter into drive and squealed tires as she pulled from the lot. Bodies, zombies, abandoned cars and other debris cluttered the streets, but Evie safely navigated through the mess until she was able to turn off to the road that would lead her to the University Airport. Her instinct was to drive fast, but instead she slowed the vehicle to a safe speed and paid close attention to the roadways to ensure she didn't hit anything that might bust a tire or cause her to wreck. Methodically, Evie looked from one side of the road to the other, then back again at the speedometer, forcing herself to keep it under forty miles per hour.

An abandoned semi blocked her way. Cautiously Evie maneuvered around it, two of her tires hopping the curb and sidewalk and slowly dropping back down with a heavy thump as she managed to clear the large vehicle. Realizing she was driving with one hand firmly clenching the steering wheel and the other still grasping her handgun, Evie slid the gun on the dash and placed her now free hand where each rested at the recommended ten and two position. Making the drive to the airport safely would be her only chance of survival. Being stranded in the city with no shelter was not a possibility.

Screams permeated the car windows and Evie turned to her left, watching helplessly as a man ran across the University Golf Course with dozens of zombies chasing him. She slowed her Ford to almost a halt as she considered taking the vehicle off-road and helping the man. If she did, she might get stuck, or if she wasn't careful she might even flip her only means of escape.

The man began running towards Evie his screams for help louder and renewed by her presence, his pleas were directed toward Evie specifically. She motioned for him to keep running, hoping he understood if he could make it to her vehicle she would, in fact, help.

The terrifying mob of zombies was quickly closing in but the man only had to make it across a ditch and up an embankment. Evie reached for her door handle so that she might jump out at the last moment and open the back door for him to jump inside, but as she did, the man slipped. He fell flat to his face and belly, and though he struggled to regain a horizontal position, the horde was upon him and the screams morphed into cries.

She swiftly turned her attention forward, and began driving again. Evie didn't look back at the man. There was nothing she could do to help him now, but maybe she could've done more. She might've also gotten herself killed, Evie reasoned. Either way, the man was now dead. Evie had watched him run to her for help and die. Her stomach turned and she gagged, holding down what could only be stomach acid.

To get her mind off the horrific scene, Evie focused on her ascent into the air and how she could accomplish acquiring a plane. She would take whatever she could steal, but she had only flown a handful of aircrafts. A Piper Cherokee, a Beech Bonanza, a Cessna and her favorite – the Mooney, were the only ones she had actual hours flying. She was certified to pilot any single engine plane, land, complex or high performance. She had been for a number of years. With her Uncle Delmont's passion for flying and having his plane at her disposal, it seemed natural that she acquired a license as soon as she was allowed. At seventeen, Evie was circling the skies above Benton, Kentucky and her uncle's passion had become that of her own.

Unfortunately, about five years ago Uncle Delmont had sold his plane when he couldn't pass his medical evaluation due to a heart condition. He'd had a quadruple by-pass and was no longer qualified by FAA regulations to be a pilot. She knew it had broken his heart, but that's why every chance she saved some extra money, she'd take the Mooney from the OSU Flying Club back home and take her mentor up in the air.

Before she even realized it, Evie was turning into the parking lot and scanning the area for threats. She shared the lot with a few other cars, including a little red Audi convertible whose owner was a very friendly man named Bill. Bill was old enough to be Evie's father, but they had bonded over their mutual love of the Mooney. He had even let her fly his little green, brown and white four-seater plane on a couple occasions. She hoped he had escaped safely, maybe even down to his house in Hilton Head where he so often flew to play golf and get away.

Evie slammed the Ford into park next to the chain link gate, which appeared to still be locked. Behind her in the parking lot near Bill's car, Evie noticed a few of the afflicted seemed to be chowing down on something or someone. She grabbed her duffel bag and gun and wondered if she would have enough of a chance to climb the fence and make it safely to the other side before drawing any unwanted attention from the zombies.

Fortunately, the monsters appeared completely engrossed in the meal they were making of what she now could see was a person, a larger man if she had to guess by the size of his big brown and white shoes. Evie recognized those shoes. They belonged to Bill. She had teased him about them a few months back saying they looked like bowling footwear. A lump formed in her throat. Poor old Bill, he was such a kind man. He deserved so much better.

As guilty as it made her feel, another thought entered her mind as quickly as the dread of realizing Bill was dead. If his body was here, so was his plane. Evie quietly opened the door of her car and peered from behind it. Three zombies were neck deep in Bill's remains. Next to him was his flight bag, which undoubtedly had the key to the gate, his hangar and his plane hooked to the loop inside.

There was no evident means of retrieving the bag without drawing the attention of the zombies. Evie skulked behind one car, then the next as she attempted to get as close as she could to her objective, the corpse of her dead friend, or more specifically, his Mooney key, all the while paying close attention to the monstrous things gobbling up his internal organs. When she closed in with only a distance of about four yards between them, one paused and began turning his head side to side in quick motions, seemingly searching the area for other prey.

Evie would need a distraction to get any closer. She considered pushing the panic button on her keyring and setting off her car alarm, but she would need to return in that direction to enter the airport. A quick survey of her surroundings lent her a possible solution to her dilemma. Instead of activating her own car alarm she would set off someone else's. Sure, she had the button to push to trigger the Ford's alarm, but a button wasn't needed. Across the lot was a new Corvette Z06. *If any car on the lot had a good alarm system, surely this one would*, Evie reasoned.

Evie gathered some broken pieces of concrete that lay on the ground around her. Patiently she waited until the zombies were absorbed with picking apart the last meaty parts of Bill. She threw the chunk of stone and held her breath in hopes that the pitch had some accuracy. As it sped through the air, the trajectory appeared to be perfect and Evie could hardly contain herself from doing a fist pump as it landed with a loud 'clink' almost dead center on the windshield. Two of the zombies raised their heads but kept picking Bill's bones. Moments passed, yet nothing happened. No screeching alarm, no flashing headlights, nothing to draw the attention of the zombies away from the flight bag that Evie so desperately needed.

She threw a rock, this time with even more force. She hit the beautiful Corvette on the hood and once again, nothing happened. Evie sighed in annoyance. She never dreamed setting off a car alarm would be so difficult. She threw another chunk of cement at a Camry close by. Again, nothing.

Unsure whether the zombies would eventually pick Bill clean and wander off or if they would find her hiding so close, Evie was unwilling to wait any longer to see what would happen. Cautiously, she crept between cars and with a stroke of luck and very stealthy movements Evie reached the Corvette and quietly crouched between it and the Camry. Bracing herself for the loud sound and dash she would have to make between more cars to Bill's body once the alarm attracted the zombies, Evie gritted her teeth. With a big exhale, she jerked on the door and to her surprise, instead of an alarm tripping, the door opened.

Frustration began to set in, however, Evie decided to check the vehicle for any supplies she might later use. With a quick peep to ensure the zombies were still preoccupied with Bill's corpse, Evie was satisfied they had no idea more food was in the area. Searching through the abandoned vehicle, Evie found very few items of any use. A pack of cigarettes and a lighter, a set of golf clubs in the back, some thread-bare chamois cloths, an iPhone and several business cards.

Evie pulled a nine iron from the golf bag. Initially she had reached for the driver, but concluded the iron might hold up better. At least she had found a makeshift weapon in her search of the vehicle, but now what? She really needed that flight bag and some distraction to get those zombies out of the way. Evie slapped herself in the forehead, and as she did, it was though she had knocked an idea loose. She laid the golf club on the ground outside the car and grabbed the chamois and the cigarette lighter. She'd seen this move in movies dozens of times, but whether it worked or not, she had no idea. She smiled as she spotted the button for the gas flap release and hit it.

Evie ripped the old chamois into strips and began tying a couple of the clothes together at the edges. She shoved the cloth in the hole of the gas tank. When several inches were in, she realized she had no real idea what she was doing and wondered how much cloth really needed to be in there for her strategy to be effective. Concluding the rag needed to be saturated, Evie used the golf club handle to jam the cloth in all the way to the knot that tied on the second piece and slid the rag back up until she spied a portion that was gas-soaked. Grabbing the golf club with her left hand, she lit the cigarette lighter with a shaky right hand and ignited the very bottom tip of the material. As soon as the rag caught fire, Evie began running as hard and fast as she could toward the vehicles she had previously been hiding behind.

As she ran, mindful to keep an eye on her zombie companions, Evie realized she hadn't been very covert in her mission to set the car on fire and sneak away. Her heavy footfalls and flailing arms hadn't exactly been inconspicuous. The idea of an exploding vehicle had frightened her more than the idea of three zombies chasing her, which they now were.

Evie made a quick turn to head in the direction of Bill's flight bag, since the zombies were no longer hovering over his carcass, but instead quickly pursuing her. Much like the feeling she had when Roslyn, the apartment complex's secretary had been chasing her, Evie could feel the closeness of one of the zombies to her back. It was faster than her and gaining. She could hear it directly behind her and imagined it reaching out and almost grasping her.

With a quick spin, Evie slung the golf club behind her and connected with the zombie's head. It immediately went down, but wasn't dead from the twitching she was witnessing. Gripping the nine iron with both hands she chopped at the zombie's head as though she had an axe in her grip. The twitching subsided, but the other two had caught up and were upon her.

Just as she readied herself to swing at the closest one, a deafening boom and fireball exploded as the Corvette was engulfed in flames frightening Evie to the point she fell to the ground, taking down the two zombies with her. She scrambled to get up and was on her feet before either of the hideous creatures. Taking advantage of her upright position Evie wasted no time and began clubbing one then the other until both their heads were little more than bloody pulp.

Evie grabbed the flight bag as she endeavored not to look at what was left of her friend and fellow pilot, Bill. Although she was far from squeamish, seeing someone she cared for so badly mutilated wasn't a sight she was sure she could stomach. She wished there was something she could do to respect Bill and hated the idea of leaving what was left of him there for other zombies to eventually stroll by and scarf down, but there was little to be done and time was of the essence.

Evie sprinted to her Ford and grabbed her duffel bag. Unwilling to leave the golf club behind since it had made such an efficient weapon, she tucked it under her armpit, shoved the handgun which she had carelessly left on the dash into the back of her pants after assuring the safety was on and began rummaging through Bill's flight bag. Just as she had expected, the keys to the fence and the hangar as well as Bill's plane were clipped to the loop inside the bag. In addition to the keys were a few handy items Evie was thankful to find. A flashlight, headset, numerous charts, logbooks and maps as were in all pilot's totes, and neatly arranged in the pockets. Evie also found a handgun, a nice pair of sunglasses and a box of ammo. She quickly zipped the tote back up and let herself through the gate. Grabbing both bags, Evie relocked the gate before hotfooting it toward Bill's plane.

Evie dropped her supplies and unlocked the hangar entrance. With very little daylight shining in the dark room, Evie felt around on the wall until she reached the button, which would open the large sliding door. Sunlight began to spread across the gloomy hangar and reveal the pretty little green, brown and white airplane. A wave of relief washed over Evie as she looked upon the aircraft knowing that she now had a real chance for survival.

The Mooney appeared pristine upon first glance. Bill took very good care of his toys. The plane was always clean and in perfect running order, as was his little convertible Audi. Evie attempted to push any memories of Bill from her mind. She had left him there in the parking lot in such an awful display and now she was stealing his plane. She wondered how many more atrocious acts she'd have to commit before she was safely back home with her family.

Evie removed the blocks from the Mooney's wheels and began pulling the plane out of the hangar. Meticulously going through each preflight check as she always did, Evie ran through the mental list of each item to inspect. Saying each thing aloud as she always did, Evie checked to find that both gas tanks were full and was about to inspect the fuel when a horrific screeching moan jerked her attention from the aircraft to the end of the runway.

Ohio State's bovine facility sat just outside of the airfield's fences. A few head of cattle had run through the fence and made it to the runway when they were caught and currently being devoured by a different kind of herd. Zombies surrounded the large cows and ripped into their hides pulling flesh and eventually soft tissue and organs in a matter of moments. Evie froze.

She had no time to finish her preflight inspection. Evie needed to be in the air immediately before those things noticed her. In a panicked haste, Evie jumped on the wing, opened the door and threw her duffel, the flight bag and the golf club inside.

She paused as a chill rushed over her body and she began to shake. One of the cows was still alive and kicking, bellowing in pain so loudly that it unnerved Evie. While the animal was still making an extreme amount of noise, Evie climbed over the few provisions she had. She slid into her seat and took a deep breath. She would normally never neglect inspecting each part of the plane and being thorough, but she felt certain that if any plane was well maintained and in top condition, it would be Bill's.

She said a silent prayer that the cow's cries of pain would distract from the sound of the aircraft, and with a resolved hand, Evie switched on the master, the electric fuel pump and listened to the whine as the electric fuel gauge came to life. She made sure the mixture was full rich and gave two pumps to the throttle. She turned the starter. A quick glance to the end of the runway proved luck to be on her side as the zombies seemed to pay no mind to the Mooney and continued to destroy the poor cow.

Evie taxied from the hangar to the far end of the runway away from the thrashing animals and zombies, glancing up at the windsock. There was a slight crosswind. She lined the spinner of the propeller to the center of the runway, added one pump of flaps for her take-off and did the quickest run-up she had ever done switching back and forth between the right and left magnetos. There was barely a drop on the tachometer. Exercising the prop, she pumped the oil into the hub. Bill had always done this three times for luck, so Evie repeated his motions in hopes of the same good fortune. One last glance down to the trim meter, she rolled the trim wheel back to the take-off position, put both feet on the brakes and fire-walled the throttle. This would be a high-performance take-off. As the plane shook and strained against the brakes, the tachometer read two thousand, seven hundred RPM.

She paused for only a moment as she gazed at the horror at the end of the runway. Mesmerized by the carnage that was once a docile cow, her stomach flipped. Large chunks of hide were missing and the zombies pulled at the animal's strands of muscle and organs as they gorged themselves.

One of the zombies looked up from the meal that was quickly becoming unrecognizable. The creature appeared to have once been a woman, Evie assumed, by the stringy, long hair that was now matted with blood. It finished chewing the gore that was being shoveled from her hand to her mouth and uncomfortably cocked her head as she stared toward Evie and the Mooney suddenly interested in something other than her meal of raw beef.

The unnerving showdown set Evie into motion. A terror overcame her and she quickly released the brakes of the shuddering aircraft. As she steered with the rudder pedals straight at the staring zombie, it rose from the carcass and began shambling toward the plane. Seconds later, two more followed.

A bizarre game of chicken commenced. The zombies began running full speed toward the Mooney, and Evie began speeding toward them full-throttle wondering, praying that she'd have enough runway to take off.

The creatures were growing larger in her sight, their features becoming clear. In a matter of yards the plane's prop would hit them, hopefully chopping them all to bits if it did, but also leaving Evie stranded with a grounded plane and waiting to die.

The zombies grew closer and closer. Evie wanted to shut her eyes but she stared straight ahead, waiting for that familiar feeling that finally came. The air speed indicator reached sixty, minimum takeoff speed. She hesitated only a moment, and pulled back slowly but surely on the yolk as the plane broke ground. She pulled back even more, hoping her climb rate would clear the zombies. As she began this steep climb up, she noticed her airspeed begin to drop. With each of her flights with Bill, he had always repeated, "the minute you break ground get the wheels up, get the flaps up, and get this baby cleaned up," and she knew exactly what needed to be done.

She eased up on the yolk, pushing it forward just slightly to gain speed. The zombies would soon be a distant memory and she was finally safely in the air. Evie pulled the throttle back to twenty-five inches and the prop back to twenty-five hundred RPM. She could now do a cruise climb to altitude to get back home. She had made it.

She could no longer see the zombies, only clouds as she rose above the airstrip, above the annihilated city that she had grown to love and above to the safety and comfort that she needed more than anything.

Evie laughed.

CHAPTER THREE

Evie had been floating for about an hour. That's what she thought to herself. Flying a small plane wasn't like taking a commercial airliner. It was like floating in the sky. No other feeling was quite like it. She truly loved being above everything that caused her stress. It had been the only thing that had calmed her during her tedious years of medical school. The sky was her safe haven. Now it literally was.

The gratefulness she felt for her uncle was unmatched by any other emotion. Her ability to pilot an aircraft had been all that had saved her. In just over an hour she would be landing back in her hometown, away from the crazy streets of Columbus to a security she would have nowhere else.

Evie knew to divide her attention between the inside of her aircraft and the outside. She watched for other planes, hopeful for any sign of life. She checked her gauges and she had tried reaching out on the radio to anyone within earshot, but received no response. Port Columbus airport was unresponsive, as was any other airport she attempted to contact. Evie's curiosity was brimming, but she dared not land or even lower her altitude until she reached her destination. *"Altitude is your friend,"* her Uncle Delmont would always say, yet Evie wondered if the rest of the world was infected.

Although she had already killed, not only strangers, but also her own roommate, Evie began asking herself if those who were bitten could possibly be cured. It seemed improbable, since she was certain that the virus that had caused their zombie-state had also seemed to kill them. They were in fact, dead already. Even her respected attending physician, Dr. Stillman, had concurred with this diagnosis. He had stated on television that those who were sick, weren't sick at all, but in fact reanimated corpses.

Evie shook her head. *Was any of this really possible?* Her entire life for the last several years had been based around her knowledge of human anatomy and physiology. A truly dead person didn't come back to life, at least not like this. Sure, she had witnessed heart attack victims being revived, a child who had drown given a second chance with CPR and things such as that, but not zombies.

What was left of those afflicted was not functioning on a normal level. There were no traces of humanity, no individuality, thought or reason. The creatures were like rabid animals, yet seemingly unfeeling of physical pain. They kept coming until they were absolutely dead, even if they were missing appendages. It was just as it seemed, crazy as it may be. Evie resigned herself to accept the fact she lived in a world where there were now zombies.

Evie switched the gas tank and gazed at the little dots on her GPS. Fortunately, it was still working and she had a relatively simple flight just following the line home. Evie let out a long sigh and stretched her shoulders. The relief of getting off the ground and finding a short reprieve of safety was beginning to wear off. Evie would have to land soon, and she had no idea what she would find or how difficult the rest of her journey would be. She was certain as long as Uncle Delmont was alive her mother and grandmother were safe as well.

Uncle Del was the closest thing to a father Evie had ever known. He had helped her mother raise her when her father had passed away when she was just a baby and had treated her like his own. Delmont was a handsome older man. In photos of his younger years, Evie had found him to be quite attractive. He wasn't too short or too tall, had a nice smile, that is, when he did smile, and a head full of dark thick hair even now that he was in his sixties. He, however, had never married or had children himself though. When Evie asked him why, he explained that his high school sweetheart hadn't wait for him when he was sent to Vietnam. When he had returned, she had gotten hitched to another man, but that was okay with him, he had told Evie. When Del was in Vietnam, he found his one true love... flying. Stationed in Chu Lai, Uncle Del had first worked on helicopters, but his love of all things that could fly only grew. He had gotten his pilot's license, owned a plane and taught Evie everything that she knew. *Thank goodness for Uncle Del,* Evie thought.

Time slipped away as Evie examined her thoughts. Cruising along, Evie was shocked to find she already had sight of Kentucky Lake a short distance ahead. The dot on her GPS that read "M34," the

Kentucky Dam Airport identifier, was very close. Evie decided to take a quick peek at the condition of the runway, since, if Uncle Delmont hadn't mowed his grass landing strip, she'd need to fly back there to land anyway.

Picking up the radio, Evie spoke clear and concise.

"Kentucky Dam Traffic, Mooney Niner One Seven ten miles northeast, inbound for landing. Any other aircraft in area? If so, please respond on this frequency, Mooney Niner One Seven."

Evie waited. There was no response.

"Kentucky Dam Unicom, anybody home?"

Again nothing.

Evie's stomach knotted. She began thinking back to one of her courses that covered epidemics. Typhus, measles, yellow fever, the bubonic plague all took time to become widespread. However, she wasn't dealing with anything like those. With such a short incubation period and the patients being fully symptomatic, as zombies within a few hours, a plague of this type could be global almost immediately with no recourse for the CDC or anyone else to do anything. She said a silent prayer that her hometown was untouched, but she expected the worst.

Her feelings were confirmed as she began her descent and noticed a complete lack of any traffic on Interstate 24. Normally, this would be a busy route. Instead of attempting to land at Kentucky Dam Airport, Evie changed course a little further to the south and began flying to her uncle's. The trek of a few short miles in Columbus from her apartment to Don Scott field at the Ohio State University campus had been treacherous and she had encountered numerous zombies. There was no way she wanted to land fifteen miles from her destination with no guarantee of finding a car. Trying to make it on her own to her mother's home would be impossible on foot and with limited ammo. She would land at Uncle Del's and hopefully find him so that the two of them could go out together and reach her mother and grandmother. If things were as bad in Benton as they had been in Columbus, they would need to make haste. Uncle Delmont's would be safe. His cabin was essentially an arsenal stocked full of guns and ammo. Her mother and grandmother, however, had only one shotgun and lived in town.

Suddenly, Evie became sick with worry. She hadn't considered her rural hometown being overrun with the infected quite like Columbus had been. She needed to believe her family was safe.

Within minutes, Evie flew in her normal pattern over Uncle Del's. As she descended, she circled giving herself a good view of the landing strip and the surrounding area. Uncle Del's windsock indicated her direction to land was good, and she prepared herself to once again be on the ground.

Her heart jumped in her throat and tears rushed down her face as Evie spotted the one thing she had prayed for the most. Uncle Del and her mother were running across his field, arms waving, and just as she had hoped, Uncle Delmont's field was freshly mowed and in perfect condition. She could land and her family was secure.

With a couple small bumps, the Mooney glided to a smooth landing. Uncle Del motioned with both hands for Evie to taxi to his fuel pump. Of course, he would want to prepare the Mooney in case they needed to use it again. Other than getting on the ground, Evie hadn't even considered anything further than running to her mother's arms. With just enough time to shut off the engine and push her way through the door, Evie bolted from the plane to meet her family.

"Great landing, Hot Rod!" Del beamed in a prideful tone and threw his arms around the girl.

"Is it down here? What's happening?" Evie questioned.

Before she could get a response, Uncle Delmont pushed her to the ground and raised his shotgun.

Evie's mother rushed to the girl and grabbed her up, wrapping her in her arms and placing one hand over an ear just in time to muffle the loud bang.

Evie spun in the direction of her uncle's shot to see a figure fall just to the other side of the grass airstrip where Evie had helped her uncle lay drainage tiles years ago.

"Damn things try to eat you! I've never seen anything like it!" Del shouted.

"Where's Grandma Birdie?" Evie asked her mother.

"She's inside. We are all safe. Let's go back in before more of those people come looking for us. The noise seems to draw them out," Retta, Evie's mom, whispered as though more of the zombies would hear.

"Those ain't people, Retta. We've been over this," Uncle Del declared in frustration. "Evie, you need to talk some sense into your mama, she thinks these things are still people. I had to kill what used to be Cordie Edwards this morning. She was beating on your mama's windows and all shambling about like a rabid 'coon does."

"Mother, he's right. I'm not sure how this happened or how it all makes sense, but the ones infected aren't people anymore. You can't believe Uncle Del killed Miss Cordie," Evie reasoned.

"Infected? How'd these folks get infected?" Uncle Del asked.

"I don't know much, but I'll tell you what I've seen. Let's go inside where it's safe," Evie suggested.

Uncle Del took a quick look around the property with a keen eye, Evie was sure. He ushered her and her mother toward the cabin and ran back to refuel the Mooney. Evie was nervous to leave him alone, but she wanted to see her grandmother and her war vet uncle was nothing if not a survivalist.

CHAPTER FOUR

Days turned to weeks and the weeks became months. Each day was the same. The family remained quarantined from the rest of the world in Del's cabin. Word had trickled through the grapevine from the few survivors they encountered that nowhere was truly safe. When Evie first arrived, there had been a number of reports from neighbors of the masses of infected townspeople. As time went by, more of the folks she knew were leaving for the safety of their family's homes out of town and survivors who were hunkering down at their own places far outside of the city limits. Fewer and fewer of the neighbors came by to check in, until eventually no one stopped by the cabin at all. The infection was widespread and Evie began to wonder how many of the people she had grown up with had actually made it. The world had changed and most of its occupants had died. It truly was an apocalypse. Del, of course, was in his element, and it made no sense to venture out looking for better accommodations or another refuge when they had everything they needed to survive where they were, lonely as it was.

In her time sequestered with her family, Evie had found the woods had become her sanctuary. She had become increasingly familiar with her surroundings and above all, a fairly proficient shot with any one of her uncle's guns.

The forest around her grew silent as Evie scoped out anything that might serve as dinner. Evie once believed that noises in the woods could serve as warnings, but now she understood that wasn't entirely true. The lack of noise was always more telling. The time to worry was when it's became too quiet – no birds chirping, no squirrels hopping tree to tree, no scurrying critters beneath the brush. She knew immediately she wasn't alone. The silence was deafening. Someone or something was nearby. She could feel it.

Evie hunkered down behind a large tree trunk. She didn't move and scarcely breathed. The Benelli shotgun would hardly serve her new purpose, so she quietly laid it under a wild berry bush. She slid her uncle's Glock 9mm out of the waistband in the back of her pants and flipped off the safety. Minutes seemed to pass like days and finally she heard it. The telltale sign of Evie's company approached. It was no more than a twig snapping and the faint sound of leaves crunching underfoot, but it was clearly not animal.

She peered around the tree trunk using the berry bush as cover. Evie's presence wasn't completely unnoticed by her woodland companion either, because he was obviously attempting to move stealthily as well. Unfortunately for her, he was a mammoth of a man, around six and a half foot, certainly not someone she would want to have to go hand to hand with in a fight for her life. Unfortunately for him, his back was turned to Evie, and she was armed.

She carefully, but quickly advanced the few feet that separated her from the giant man until he became aware of her, but it was too late.

"Don't move," Evie growled.

She held the Glock to the back of his neck since she couldn't reach his head comfortably. She'd hoped to disguise her voice to sound like a large man as well, but as soon as the words escaped her mouth, Evie knew she hadn't. By the angle and location of the gun barrel, he'd more than likely already figured she was smaller and female.

"Now, drop the rifle," Evie continued.

"Don't shoot. I've got a family. I'm just trying to hunt. You can take my squirrels, but don't kill me," the voice sounded all too familiar and although Evie hadn't socialized with hardly anyone but family in Western Kentucky for years before the plague hit, she doubted too many Goliath sized men had migrated to the rural area.

"Trevor? Is that you?"

"That depends. If it is, are you going to shoot me?" He asked.

Evie lowered her gun and kicked him in the backside. "You big idiot, you almost scared me out of my wits!"

"You're the one with the gun, Evie Stone!" He laughed, a little too loud and they both began scanning the area for anyone within earshot.

"Well, it's good to see you alive. So your family's okay then?" Evie asked hesitantly, she rarely ever ran into other survivors, and conversation was even more rare.

"Yeah, we're good. My wife, you remember Vickie? She was visiting her father in Georgia, I haven't heard from her since it all started, but the girls are good. All three," he smiled from ear to ear as he mentioned his daughters.

Trevor's demeanor changed as he spoke of his girls. The imposing man became a giant teddy bear grinning like he could hardly contain the joy at just the mention of his children.

Evie had always found Trevor attractive, mostly because of his kind ways. At least, she had always assumed that, yet seeing him beam with pride over his children made her realize his kindness wasn't the only thing that made him handsome. His piercing dark eyes became warm and his smile inviting. Evie smiled back at him and for the first time in months actually felt some semblance of happiness and normality.

The two walked for a short while together, catching up and sharing gossip until Trevor had to go one way and Evie the other. He hugged her tight, and the old friends parted ways. He lived only a few miles away from Uncle Del's hunting cabin, but chances were slim she'd see him again anytime soon. A chance meeting in the woods had made her day yet left her as empty as before.

Evie and Trevor had tried dating during the summer before her freshman year of college. There had always been some attraction to the boy, but where his looks had been abundant to Evie, he had lacked as much in ambition. She'd eventually broken his heart when she went to school and ended the relationship. Of course, Evie had big plans, and Trevor wanted to stay in West Kentucky. He had begun working for and eventually taken over the family construction business. Funny how things turned out, she thought. Her big plans were worthless now, just like her college degree. She was back in Kentucky and Trevor was better off than she would ever be from learning something useful like how to build things.

Seeing him again turned out to be the straw that broke the camel's back. It was getting dark, and Evie knew her family would start to worry but she slumped down at the edge of the woods and quietly sobbed. She hadn't cried since the outbreak. All her life's plans were useless. She'd spent so much time and money learning to save people, yet there were no saving people now. The only doctoring she'd had the opportunity to do was wrapping Uncle Del's sprained ankle when he had fallen a few days earlier.

In the months that had passed, no one had shared any new knowledge of what had happened. Theories ran from government conspiracies to the end of days and hell on earth. The last of the information came with the end of the media coverage. It had been obvious there were survivors, the ones that were still truly alive, not the rotters that scratched at her family's door in the night when they made too much noise. Evie had seen a few humans stealing and killing during daylight hours as she cautiously watched from safety. Some of Benton's residents had been shot for nothing more than the equivalent of a couple bags of groceries, and she could do nothing to stop it. Del had warned her that the looting, rioting and killing would start shortly after she arrived, and he had been correct. It didn't take her long to realize she could trust no one short of her family and staying in the shadows was their only hope of survival. Del had forbade her to venture close to town, and even though she didn't like being told what to do, she had to agree. It was entirely too dangerous to be out in the open.

Up until this moment, Evie had felt lucky to be alive, but now she questioned whether it wouldn't have been so much easier if she hadn't given up log before now.

It was full dark by the time Evie returned to the cabin. Her mother and grandmother were in panic mode but Delmont was calm. He had been the one to teach Evie to shoot when she was a kid. Although Evie knew Uncle Del would have preferred a nephew to a niece, he seemed to have complete faith in her abilities. The fact she had just brought home five squirrels seemed to add to his confidence.

Since Del's unfortunate spill, Evie had become the sole provider for the group. Bringing home little more than a squirrel a day and a pocketful of berries for the last two, she had begun to doubt herself. Now Evie was comfortable in the idea that they would survive. Her aim was sharpening and her empty belly gave her incentive. Things would never be like they had been, but she could take care of herself and her family at least.

"Great job, today," Del whispered as they headed out back to clean the squirrels.

"Thanks. I had a little scare while I was out there though."

"Oh?"

"I was very careful, listening to my surroundings like you taught me when I realized I wasn't alone."

"What happened, Ev?" Del's knife stilled, his eyes no longer on the squirrel he was dressing.

"Well, I hid. Then when he got close, I got the drop on the guy and pulled the Glock on him," she smiled at the thought of having the upper hand on Trevor.

"You shot him?" Del whispered.

"No, no! It was just Trevor Thomas."

"Evelina, tell me you didn't tell him where we were. You know we can't feed any more mouths around here."

"Of course not, Uncle Del. Besides he seemed to be doing fine on his own."

Uncle Del seemed appeased, but Evie hadn't been expecting such a harsh reaction from him. She hadn't considered what he'd said. They really couldn't afford to feed anyone else. The family was scrapping to get by as it was, and Evie wasn't sure she could turn Trevor and his three small girls away.

They finished skinning the squirrels in silence and took them inside for Retta and Birdie to cook. After dinner Evie settled in her spot by the fireplace and began to read an Edith Wharton novel she'd already read twice before. Entertainment was at a minimum. Uncle Delmont cleaned his shotgun, and her mother and grandmother reminisced as they looked through old photos. That had become the family's evening ritual.

Retta, Del's younger sister by a decade, was in her late fifties, yet had inherited the blessed genetics of their mother Birdie, who was now eighty-three. Both women appeared years younger than they were and shared the same bright blue eyes and silver hair.

As much as Evie's mother and grandmother favored physically, the two were also remarkably the same in their personalities as well. Not a soul in Benton had a bad word to speak of either woman. When they weren't taking dinners to the sick, they were volunteering at the soup kitchen. Evie had always been so thankful to have such sweet female role models, but attributed her spunky streak to her uncle.

The first few nights after Evie had gotten back it had seemed like heaven, being with her loved ones, having the stability and security of her family. The journey from Columbus, Ohio to Western Kentucky had been nothing short of hell by herself not knowing what she would find or if her family was alive.

She remained mostly grateful that she lived through the travel, but Evie had begun to contemplate where life would take her. Her family lived day to day, protecting each other, hunting for food, boiling water to drink. Everyone had chores and they managed to endure. But it was just the four of them. Would this be all she ever had to look forward to? She felt horribly guilty for even having the thought, but she hoped at some point she would at least have a friend again. She hoped for more.

Throughout medical school, her studies had always come first. Her education left little time for fun. Evie had always been considered a bit of a nerd in high school, but college had been a different story. The other students had admired her work ethic and guys began noticing her. She would get asked out on dates somewhat regularly and Evie's confidence had grown. She had always assumed once she had gotten past the stress of school and her first year of residency, she'd have plenty of time to find the right guy. Instead, the only single man she'd been around in months was her uncle and her hopes of finding a future husband seemed slim. She regretted not listening to her Grandma Birdie's advice of not becoming an "old maid." The lack of eligible bachelors lended little to no promise of a future where she wasn't alone. Evie couldn't be sure if there were any decent single men left in this new plagued world.

Each evening Del would turn on his flight radio and check for other survivors. The radio had a signal that would reach around one hundred and fifty miles. Each night he received the same response. Nothing. The family had discussed taking the Mooney to find other survivors and a place that might be safer, yet Del and her mother always agreed. Nowhere would ever be as safe as their home.

CHAPTER FIVE

Evie finally dozed to sleep and was dreaming of chocolate cheesecake and sweet red wine when she was violently jerked awake. It was still dark when a hand roughly covered her mouth and nose, waking her from a dead sleep. Before she could react, her Uncle Del whispered in her ear.

"Be very quiet. Someone is outside."

Evie was certain that now was definitely one of those times when Uncle Del would have preferred a nephew. She blinked her eyes awake, and quietly slid the 9mm from under her pillow. Evie looked to her uncle and he motioned her toward the bedroom door where Retta and Birdie were sleeping, silently telling her to join the other women. Evie shook her head and mouthed "no" and pointed to him.

Del narrowed his eyes at her, but when she motioned to his ankle, he reluctantly complied. His injury would prohibit him from helping much. Slowly, he opened the bedroom door wide enough to slip inside and crouched underneath the window, gun ready.

Evie crept toward the front door, but it was Del's turn to shake his head. He nodded toward the small patio door off the tiny living area of his cabin. Of course, he was right to stop her. The sliding door would be quiet, and offered an exit that would be less conspicuous. Taking a deep breath, Evie steeled her nerves and carefully unlatched the patio door, sliding it slowly across the track in an effort to make no sound.

She peeped out in both directions, but saw nothing. Evie squeezed through the small slit she'd made into the night air and slid along the outside wall of the cabin so cautiously it seemed like days before she came to the corner.

Evie dreaded going any further, though she knew she must. She prayed she wouldn't have to kill anyone. She had entered medical school to save lives. She didn't want to have to take any. Her heart was pounding so fast and hard she could hear it in her ears. This particular side of the house had no windows. It would be a blind spot for Del. He wouldn't be able to cover her at all. She was on her own.

Evie took a deep breath and ducked low, aiming the gun all around like she'd seen detectives do on television when they would burst through a suspect's door. So far she'd seen no sign of movement, but she knew without a doubt someone had to be close. Evie trusted her uncle, and if he was certain someone was there, she was certain about his instincts.

Whispered voices permeated the warm summer air. Although she couldn't clearly hear what they said, she knew two things. There was more than one intruder on their property and the trespassers were definitely up to no good. A normal person who meant no harm would surely knock at the door, especially in rural Kentucky where the residents were, for the most part, armed and knew how to properly fire a weapon.

Uncle Del had taught Evie to be quiet back in her youth when they would hunt. She gingerly stepped around the shrubbery that lined his cabin, warily attempting to remain behind the cover of the bushes to obstruct the intruder's view should they actually hear her. Leaves lightly crunched under her feet, and she paused terrified that the unwelcome visitors might become aware of her presence. She took a deep breath and held it, listening closely to anything that might give away their position.

Some twigs snapped and two shadowy figures appeared around the edge of the house that Evie faced. She crouched behind a fat shrub and rested her wrists atop the small limbs as she aimed at one of the men.

"This is Del Tucker's cabin," one of the men surmised.

"If he's in there, you know he's packing," the other cautioned.

"Let's head on over to the Reyburn's farm down the road and check for supplies. We can come back here during the day and see if Old Del is still above ground."

"Good idea, Guardrail."

The two men took one last look around and made their way through the wood until they were out of sight. Evie was relieved to see them leave, but at the same time sick to her stomach that they would be coming back. She knew one of them, and he had been trouble since elementary school.

When she knew it was safe to move, Evie crept back around the cabin to the sliding door she had exited earlier and quietly shut it behind her. Del flashed an inquiring look and she noticed her mom, as well as her grandmother, were both awake and waiting to hear what she had witnessed.

"There were two of them. They left," Evie whispered as though she was still frightened of being overheard by the dangerous men.

"What were they doing?" Del asked.

"Recon, I think. Looking for supplies. They knew you owned this place and decided to come back in the daylight to make sure it was safe. They said they knew you would be armed."

"Darn right, I'm armed," Del answered.

"They were SOC," Evie added.

A long sigh released from her uncle's lips.

"What's SOC?" Grandma Birdie questioned.

"Soldiers of Chaos. The motorcycle gang. When I ran into Larry Johnson hunting over by the bottoms a couple weeks ago, he told me they had taken over the west side of town. We're going to need to watch our backs."

The family eventually returned to their beds, but Evie doubted any of them slept. She could hear her grandmother whispering questions about their safety to her mother, and her uncle periodically limped around to each window and peered into the darkness outside. Whether or not the Soldiers would actually try to do them harm and steal their supplies was a real crapshoot. It depended highly on what they'd scavenged the night before and which of the members came to the house, and of course how drunk they were, she reasoned. She was familiar with most of them, some were just rough, but others were downright mean.

Evie had grown up with a few of them. Desmond Young, or Des, was in many of her accelerated placement classes in school up until his parents died and his uncle, Priest, took him in. Priest was the leader of the Soldiers of Chaos. After that, Evie rarely saw Desmond in school until one day she'd heard he had quit. By the time they should've graduated high school Evie only saw him drinking, smoking and riding motorcycles with Damien Garland, who everyone referred to as "Guardrail." She always wanted to talk to Des, but Guardrail and his horrible skank of a girlfriend, Danielle, seemed to always be around, so she never bothered. Dani, as they called her, hated Evie, and she was the type who might just stab you in the face if you looked at her wrong. Des and Guardrail were among the new generation of the biker crew and even though she rarely spoke with anyone from her high school, she had still heard stories about them.

When dawn finally broke, Uncle Del and Evie decided instead of holding down the fort, the time had come to leave. Down the road past the Reyburn's farm was a hunting shack Mr. Reyburn used during deer season and they would stay there overnight with the intention of going into town and finding some allies in the next few days. Uncle Del had some good friends who had survived since last he'd heard. Del would be an asset to anyone once his ankle was healed, so Evie felt certain that anyone they came by would be glad to see them. Few were as good a shot and he would easily be able to provide meat. However, with his injury and the fact that Evie's mother and grandmother were in tow, they were at a disadvantage should the Soldiers of Chaos come back looking for trouble. They had decided their odds weren't good if it came to a standoff with a motorcycle gang.

The family packed up as many supplies as they could carry. Uncle Del could barely walk, but with Retta's help, he hobbled through the woods. Evie could tell he was in pain and asked frequently if he needed to stop and rest, but he always refused, and her mother seemed to have him under control. Evie went ahead of the group, scouting for rotters, gang members or any other trouble that might be waiting for them. Fortunately, it was quiet.

Through the trees, Evie spotted the Reyburn's farmhouse. A pickup truck and two Harleys sat outside. Evie and her family squatted behind some brush and watched the doors in silence. Within a few minutes, Priest, who had significantly aged since Evie had last seen him, appearing feeble and more like Desmond's grandfather than uncle, strolled out of the home. Another biker, a heavy set boy they called Chicken, followed Priest outside carrying some garbage bags and rode away.

"Do you think they know about the cabin?" Evie whispered.

"Not many people knew about that place," Uncle Del replied.

"Do you think Mr. Reyburn had any supplies stocked in it?" Evie asked hopefully.

"Hard to say, when they took off for their kin's place in Tennessee he probably took most stuff, but we have all we need for now. Don't get any ideas about looting. We only take what we need."

"Oh no!" Retta cried, entirely too loudly.

Evie began to survey their surroundings hoping the outburst hadn't drawn any attention.

"What's wrong?" Birdie mouthed to her daughter.

"We forgot our photo album!" Retta sobbed.

"I'll go back and get it," Evie offered.

Her mother, Uncle Del as well as Evie's grandmother all quietly, but adamantly whispered "no."

"I will make sure no one is around and I can be quick."

Retta repeatedly shook her head, but Uncle Del seemed to think about what Evie had said for a few moments.

"Leave what you have here and double back now. We will wait a little while and see if there is any more funny business at the Reyburn house. When it gets quiet, I'll get your mama and grandma to the cabin. Do like I showed you, walk softly, be aware of your surroundings and if you see or hear anything that isn't a rotter, hide. If you see a rotter, get away or try to bean 'em with your bat. Only use the gun as a last resort. You aren't just avoiding rotters, Hot Rod, you need to avoid people."

"She is not leaving!" Retta argued.

"She goes out hunting for us every day. She made it over four hundred miles to get back to us with no one's help. Our girl is resourceful."

Evie smiled, but it quickly fell from her face as she saw the angry look on her mother's. Instead of waiting for permission, Evie dropped her backpack, shotgun and checked the Glock. It was loaded and ready, so she pulled her baseball bat from her pack and began darting from tree to tree and quickly, yet quietly making her way through the woods backtracking to Del's cabin. Bird's chirped and squirrels scurried along the way and Evie began to lose focus as she neared her destination and headed down Uncle Del's gravel drive toward the front door of the cabin.

The sound of rumbling motorcycles whisked her back into reality. She quickly dove behind Uncle Del's woodpile. With her back to the small house, resting against the uneven ricks of wood, Evie held the Glock against her chest and barely took a breath as the bikes pulled up the narrow, wooded drive.

Peeping between the holes of the stacked wood, Evie saw two motorcycles, and three people. Desmond, Guardrail and behind him the deplorable Dani were climbing off the bikes and pulling large canvas totes from the saddlebags. Dani looked around and stared straight in Evie's direction for some time. Evie became convinced the dirty slut had spotted her. Evie's hands shook and she gritted her teeth in anticipation for trouble, but Dani finally looked away. The perma-scowl on her face apparently meant nothing more than it was Tuesday, not that she had seen Evie hiding.

"You think Old Del is around? Dead or alive in there?" Guardrail asked.

"We will knock and find out. Don't go busting up in there unless you wanna get shot," Desmond replied.

"He'd be the one zombie that could fire a gun!" Guardrail chortled.

Dani cackled in her deep, almost manly voice and Evie remembered exactly how uncouth the girl really was, not that it wasn't obvious from her dried out and split purple hair.

"Hey, you remember Evie, his niece, Des? She was one hot piece of tail for a nerdy chick. I'd have hit that," Guardrail joked.

Evie rolled her eyes and gritted her teeth a little harder. Every ounce of her wanted to jump up and shoot Guardrail in the crotch.

"Brother, don't talk about her. She was nice. One of the few people in this town that actually was kind to me when my parents died. Besides, she'd have never hooked up with the likes of you," Des smiled.

"Oh, you think that uppity bitch is better than me?" Dani screamed.

"On every level. Shut up before I slap your mouth shut," Desmond answered in a dangerous tone.

The three knocked on the door of the cabin and when no one answered, Guardrail broke the door down with a kick, and they disappeared inside.

Evie smiled at what Desmond had said. It was sweet of him to defend her, yet she was a little more than perturbed that he had threatened to hit a woman and had broken into her uncle's home. He was definitely much different than the sweet, smart boy she had grown up with in all those AP classes. He had become like his uncle, a formidable man. Maybe even more deadly than his uncle, because Desmond was smart.

The sound of things falling off shelves and breaking unnerved Evie. Del had been the only father Evie had known since she was a small child. The idea of someone trashing his home infuriated her. She began to jump up and stop them, but then Evie rationalized, she was outnumbered and no doubt outgunned. It would be a terrible idea, so she waited as she bitterly listened to more of Del's belongings break.

Finally the two men emerged with filled bags and began to load their bikes.

"Dani, come on you dumb whore," Desmond shouted.

"Look what I found. Old Del's family album full of pictures of your precious Evie," Dani mocked.

Evie hoped the disgusting girl wouldn't take the one thing she had actually come back to retrieve.

Instead, Dani ripped a photo from one of the pages and began laughing.

"Look Des, your girlfriend is all dolled up with one of those graduation outfits on. Lot of good college did that fancy bitch, she's probably dead now."

With the back of his hand, Desmond hit Dani so hard in the mouth her feet flew out from under her. When she landed, Dani spit blood. Desmond jerked the photo from her hand and held it in front of Dani's face.

"This girl, this one," he shook the photo inches from the skank on the ground, "she was smart, good and beautiful. Nothing like you. If she is dead, then this world has gone to hell, because she deserves to be alive far more than you. Don't ever say her name to me again. Do you hear me?"

Dani nodded her head and Evie noticed Desmond discreetly slid her photo in his back pocket before he jumped on his motorcycle and sped away.

"Why didn't you defend me?" Dani screamed at her boyfriend as she scrambled on the gravel to stand.

"Why do you push buttons all the time, woman? Shut yer mouth or I'll slap it closed too."

Evie waited for some time after they left before she snuck up to the driveway and grabbed the photo album that Dani had thrown to the ground. Maybe her mother wouldn't notice the photo of Evie getting her bachelor's degree was missing. Really, what did it matter anyway? That biology degree was worthless now.

CHAPTER SIX

Evie reached the tiny shack in Mr. Reyburn's woods. There her mother and grandmother shared a tiny cot that should've never accommodated two people and her uncle had made him and Evie a pallet on the floor. She hunkered down for the night, stretching out as comfortably as possible, yet laid awake. Thoughts raced through her mind, most of them about Desmond Young.

He had changed almost as much as his uncle since Evie had last seen him, but not in such a negative way. His face had slimmed, his jawline was sharp now and he looked like a man, not so much like the boy she remembered. His dirty blonde hair had grown long and shaggy. Des had also put on some serious muscle weight. No longer a stringy kid, he looked strong and in good shape. He looked hot. Evie smacked herself on the forehead for the thought.

Sure, she hadn't seen anyone her own age with the exception of Trevor in weeks, but she obsessed over what Desmond had said about her. Then of course, her brain jumped to him hitting that rat-faced Danielle, which honestly, was something Evie would love to do herself, but she couldn't excuse him for being violent with a woman. Dani, was many things, all of them absolutely loathsome, but she didn't deserve to be slapped down like he had done.

Noises from outside the cabin transported Evie back to reality. They were terrifying. A group of rotters straggled by. The family remained quiet and managed to go unnoticed. Uncle Del had camouflaged the shack before Evie had made it back by rubbing a rotted deer carcass around the perimeter. Somehow the undead seemed to smell the living otherwise, and rotter's hearing seemed almost superhuman. One had to stay very quiet to go unnoticed, so much as a muted cough or sneeze would attract them.

Evie didn't sleep at all that night. When morning finally came, she was thoroughly exhausted, but ready to go into town. She'd had enough of being in the middle of nowhere and lying around on hard floors, terrified of being eaten every night.

They packed up the blankets and water bottles and set foot on their journey. Benton, Kentucky was a small town of around just four thousand before the plague, but it had a few multiple-story buildings including a city hall and a jail, which could offer more protection than being alone in the woods.

Evie's family stuck to fields and side roads for most of the trip. Uncle Del's cabin was only about five miles outside of town by road, but they needed to stick to more rural areas with less of a chance to run into the afflicted. That's what they originally called them on the television stations. Afflicted. Evie found the name funny. The ones she had seen were ravenous monsters, hardly poor souls with an affliction.

The only way to permanently kill them was to injure their brain. Any trauma to the head that would kill a living person worked, and most of the time it took less force. Many of them were decomposing now and easy to stab, especially through an eye socket. The longer they carried the virus, the more decayed they became. However, Evie had found that the best way to avoid being bitten or scratched was to hit them with something long and to keep as much distance as possible. Her current weapon of choice was an old aluminum bat she had left at her uncle's when he taught her to play baseball as a child. A knife through the eye worked well, but that technique brought her closer than she cared to be to their mouths. A bite by one of them was a death sentence. The victim would become sick, nauseated and typically died within a matter of hours. She had witnessed it with Sheena and that timeline and symptoms had been confirmed by other survivor's accounts.

When she left her apartment, Evie had fortunately had enough sense to pack up her medical supplies. She had been certified as an EMT years back and had her portable mask on a keychain as well. Evie had worn the mask anytime she thought she might encounter one of the rotters. It helped to ensure she didn't get any of the infected blood in her mouth, eyes or any open wounds during a confrontation. She'd killed quite a few of them, and when Evie thought there were too many to fight, which was typically more than two, she hid. Her strategy had worked well, but she hadn't expected when she got back to her hometown full of good, honest small town folks that she'd be scared to be around other humans more than the zombies. People in rough times can do bad things and become very dangerous she'd learned.

The family spotted a small group of rotters on the road nearby the woods where they walked. There were only four of them, but Uncle Del and Evie were the only ones armed. They decided to let them pass and the four remained hidden in the dense brush, crouching quietly until the herd had shambled out of sight.

Evie could hardly wait to see other people and have some company other than her family. She loved them each dearly, but they'd run out of things to talk about long ago.

By afternoon, they had made it to the bridge by the old radio station. Town lay just over the hill. Evie's pace quickened and Uncle Del had to reprimand her for walking too fast for her mother and grandmother. As they crested over the hill into town, the family paused. Abandoned cars lined the streets, bodies littered the ditches and the most disturbing thing of all wasn't even the dead. A barricade of old tires, fencing and concrete blocks closed off the street. On a platform overlooking what was left of her once beautiful, now desolate hometown stood none other than Guardrail and Dani armed with rifles.

"We need to turn around," Evie whispered to Del.

"We can't. It'll be nightfall before we can get back to the cabin," Del answered.

"There's people down the street!" Evie heard Dani yell.

They were spotted. It was too late to run.

"Come on, let's just go on up there and talk to them," Del insisted.

Her uncle was cautious but Evie concluded he had no idea of the trouble and lack of intellect they were about to encounter.

Slowly, they moved forward until they stood before the barricade. Dani smiled a hateful yet toothy grin. The girl had teeth like a horse, yet stained and dark, more than likely from meth use Evie concluded. It was inevitable for any smirk of hers not to show those giant ill-arranged choppers.

"Look who's here. Miss-I'm-Better-Than-You-All. I thought you were off at your fancy ass college and hopefully dead by now," Dani drawled.

"No such luck, Dani. Those of us with an IQ over seventy have figured out ways to survive. How is it exactly you made it?" Evie sarcastically replied.

"We got no room for you here. You're gonna need to move on!" Dani screamed.

"Shut up, woman. Priest said to inform him of any survivors that came to the gate. Go tell him we have four," Guardrail ordered his girlfriend.

"Screw that. I say we just let them die out there. She's not bringing crap to the table. She can't help us."

Dani drew her weapon and aimed it at Evie, but then began to shout incoherently. Evie only caught a few of the words before Dani disappeared behind the platform with a thud and screaming bloody murder. A moment later, Desmond appeared and began barking orders for Guardrail to open the gate.

Cautiously Evie and her family entered. Desmond greeted them once inside, before he began what seemed to Evie like an interrogation.

"You were going to school up in Ohio, correct?" He inquired.

"Yes."

"For medicine?"

"Yes," Evie answered, keeping her answers short, unsure if she should admit too much.

"What specialty?"

"I was going to be a general practioner," Evie answered.

"Good," Desmond stated.

"Del, you still as good a shot as ever?" Desmond directed his next question to her uncle.

"Always."

"Then you are welcome here. I'll get a place set up for your family."

"That's not your decision to make! You have to take this to Priest!" Dani argued as she lay on the ground with what appeared to be an injury to her ankle. Evie presumed where Desmond had thrown her off the platform.

Desmond cut his eyes to the girl, with a look that Evie had scarcely ever seen, nor wanted to again. Dani immediately became quiet.

"First, you will need to surrender your firearms and all weapons," Desmond continued his conversation with her uncle.

"No disrespect son, but that's not going to happen," Del asserted.

"If you want to stay, it has to. We have rules here. I can ensure your safety inside these walls."

Not wanting to get thrown out, Evie laid her baseball bat to the ground. Guardrail was quick to pick it up. Del followed suit and relinquished his guns. Guardrail began patting Evie down and Desmond did the same to her uncle.

"Hey perv, lay off!" Evie shouted when the dirty biker began to grope her backside, not so much because the man was getting handsy, but because he was about to find her long hunting knife she had concealed. He'd already removed her Glock and Evie had no intention of losing any more of her weapons.

"Enough," Desmond warned his buddy.

Seemingly satisfied with their search, not even considering that her mother or grandmother might be stashing anything, the two stepped back and Desmond looked the family up and down one last time.

"Everyone here has a job. If I remember right from school, you ladies made some hella good desserts when class parties came around. You two can help with the cooking. Head over to Hazel's diner and find out what you can do to help out for dinner tonight. Del, you will need to help with the hunting and patrols. Guardrail is on duty now, but Jug has the night patrol. You can come back here in about an hour or so before nightfall and he can fill you in on how we do things. Evie, I'm going to need you to come with me. Now."

Evie turned to her uncle and mom, who seemed hesitant for her to leave their sides. She, too, was unsure why she needed to be separated from her family or what it was that Des had in mind for her to contribute.

"Does she need attention first?" Evie pointed to Dani, stalling.

"Skank, are you ok, or do you want the doc to check you out?" Desmond asked.

"I'd rather die first," Dani grumbled.

"I'll remember that," Evie replied with a grin on her face.

"Your guns will be returned when you leave, for now they will be put up. Only those on patrol have weapons inside of the barricade. You will all be fine. You have my word. Follow me," Des seemed to demand more than ask.

Desmond pointed out what used to be an old gift shop to the left and told Evie's family they could rest and settle in there. They would be the only ones in residence for that building. Evie wondered if anyone else had been living there. If maybe previous occupants had died and left the building vacant, but she said nothing, only following Desmond closely as her family cautiously entered the glass door of the gift shop.

Evie turned to check on her family and noticed Del give her a nod toward her backside. He knew the bikers had missed her hunting knife and was reminding her to use it should she need.

"I'm really glad to see you are doing okay," Evie spoke softly.

"I was just thinking of you, actually. I'm glad you made it too," Des grinned and for a moment almost forgot that she was having a conversation with a dangerous man, not the classmate she once knew.

"Where are we going?" Evie asked.

"We are going to see my uncle. What you see here, you will keep to yourself. You get me?" Desmond asked with a slightly threatening tone and Evie suddenly remembered exactly who he had become.

"I get it. I'm cool."

His paced quickened and the two stalked past Hazel's Diner. The door was propped open and the smell of meat grilling wafted across her nose. Evie slowed, her mouth hanging open as she was met with a furious attack.

"Evie!"

The tiny Hazel, proprietor of the diner, wrapped her arms around Evie and greeted her with a huge bear hug.

Hardly more than five foot tall, the now gray-haired Hazel was a welcome surprise. Evie had rarely made it into town during her visits from college, and each time she flew in her mother and grandmother would cook a huge meal, so it had been years since Evie had been to Hazel's restaurant. In that time, Hazel's hair had lightened, but few other things about the woman was any different. She seemed just as lively and young as ever.

Hazel had been a classmate of Retta's and the two had always been very friendly. When Evie was a child, the little woman would always give her free pie. Evie had also noticed she did the same every time her uncle frequented the diner as well. She'd always had an inclining that Hazel was a bit sweet on Uncle Del, but of course, her gruff uncle never seemed to notice.

"You're alive!" Hazel beamed.

"Oh, Hazel! It's so good to see you! Uncle Del and my mom will be so happy!"

"Enough with the reunion ladies. We've got somewhere to be, Evie. Come on," Desmond growled.

Evie waved to Hazel and sprinted to catch up with Desmond already several yards down the street. He walked extremely fast and his long legs made his gait hard for Evie to catch.

"You know, you don't have to be such a grump, Des," Evie joked.

"If you haven't noticed, it's the end of the world. I think I've earned the right to be an ass. I find your chipper demeanor a little more than annoying."

So much for small talk, Evie thought. She once considered Desmond somewhat of a friend, but those days were apparently long past. The scene at her uncle's cabin still confused her though. *Why had he defended her if he didn't like her?*

Once they passed the old grocery, Desmond turned and began walking up the sidewalk of what had once been the Health Department.

"So this is my job then? I'm going to work in here and be the town doctor?" Evie asked.

"This is where my uncle stays. Enough questions. Just follow me."

The lobby was wrecked. Empty beer bottles, sodas and cans of food littered the floor and one of the waiting room couches now appeared to be a makeshift bed with tattered blankets scattered across it.

"Priest?" Des bellowed.

"Back here," a voice cried out.

Down the hall in the last room, Evie found Desmond's uncle, Priest, sprawled out along an exam table looking clammy and sick. He appeared even more decrepit than he had when Evie had seen him at a distance the previous day.

"What the hell are you doing bringing her here?" Priest croaked.

"She's a doctor. She won't breath a word of this, will you Evie?" Des asked.

"I still believe in confidentiality. Whatever is wrong with you will stay between us," Evie reassured.

"It better or I will end you, little girl," Priest threatened.

Evie took a deep breath, gritted her teeth and clenched her fists.

"Look, if you want help, you will not threaten me. You will not treat me like some biker skank you demand obedience from and you will not demean me in any way. Are we clear, or should I leave now?"

"You little..." Priest started, but Desmond grabbed him by the shoulders and whispered in his ear.

The two laughed, Evie was sure at her expense, but the crotchety old biker seemed to settle down and even half-smiled.

"What seems to be the problem?" Evie asked.

"I'm diabetic," Priest apprehensively answered.

"How long?"

"Since I was six."

"You have Type 1. Have you been able to check your glucose and do you have access to insulin?" Evie asked.

"I've had to ration my test strips and insulin. I have a couple boxes of strips left, plenty of needles, everything I need, but I ran out of insulin yesterday. Before that I was doing about half of what I need, trying to make it last longer."

"Oh, crap. Okay, let's think about this. I'm going to assume you are in ketoacidosis. Are there any supplies left here? I need to set you up on an IV."

Priest pointed down the hallway, and Evie motioned for Desmond to come along with her.

"Your uncle isn't going to last long if we don't get some insulin soon. Have you checked all the local pharmacies?" Evie asked once they were out of earshot.

"Of course. That's what he's been using since shortly after this all happened. He has refused to let me try to go very far to loot any neighboring towns, but I'm going to head out tonight."

"I might have a better idea. Let me set him up on the IV, and I'm going to need your help."

"Anything you need. Thank you for this," Desmond responded, sounding pleasant once again.

CHAPTER SEVEN

Evie handed Desmond one file after another, throwing some to the side as she searched. Desmond held a stack of filled manila folders and wore a confounded look.

"What exactly are we doing? My uncle needs insulin tonight. I don't need to waste time with this, woman. I need to be heading out."

"I'm pulling all the files of diabetic patients in the county. We are going to go through them and see if anyone who uses insulin lives closer than Calvert City or Murray or the closest pharmacy you haven't managed to loot already. Then we will go to their house and check out their refrigerators."

"Wow. I feel a little stupid now. I never thought of that," Des smiled.

"That's what you're paying me the big bucks for, right?" Evie joked.

"Excuse me?"

"I'm the town doctor now, you guys are going to give me the biggest house and let me drive a Mercedes, right?" Evie raised her eyebrows and flashed an evil smirk.

"How about this, I'll make sure you and your family eat. I'll be sure Dani doesn't try to kill you in your sleep and on occasion, I might even bring you a present from one of our looting trips."

"Sounds fair, but I'm going to leave it open for future negotiations."

***

"Hey Priest, you feeling okay, man?" Des quietly asked his uncle, unsure whether he was awake or even conscious.

Slowly the man opened his eyes, scanned the room and pulled himself up from the exam bed. He grabbed his nephew by the collar and roughly jerked him close.

"That girl, she best not say a word about my condition, you get me?" Priest whispered.

"She won't."

"Yeah, she better not, and don't let her wear out her usefulness around here. You get what we need from her and if she even looks like she's going to cause problems, end her."

"Won't be necessary. Trust me," Desmond reassured.

"I trust no one, least of all some stuck up little city girl. Don't go getting all google-eyed over some piece."

"No worries, Uncle, but she's useful. She's trained and can take care of the people here. Give her a chance."

"One chance. If she screws up, cut her throat," Priest growled.

The grizzled old biker slapped his nephew on the back and threw himself down on the bed, pushed his pillow further under his head and nodded for Desmond to use the door and get out.

As Des opened the door, he found Evie waiting. In her dirty jeans, old t-shirt and hoodie, she still looked just a perfect as she always did at school somehow, a class above his current group of friends and club members. It had nothing to do with her education, her upbringing or her looks, but instead her as a person. She was good. Sure, he had promised his uncle if she caused problems he would take care of her, but he knew he'd never be able to bring harm to such a creature as the one who smiled at him as he stared silently back at her. As much as he fantasized about the two of them being together, he knew inside, even the end of the world wasn't enough to make that work. If he was the last man on Earth, she probably wouldn't want him, and he certainly didn't deserve her.

"What's wrong? Why are you looking at me like that?" Evie questioned.

"You look like crap. We have some fresh clothes you can grab when we get back. I know how important looking just right is to your type," he sarcastically crowed.

"What's your problem? One minute you are actually decent, then the next you turn into a giant douchebag," Evie straightened her spine and stood tall expecting to incur his wrath.

"I'll be sure to stay a giant douchebag so I don't confuse you anymore. Come on, we're wasting time."

***

Evie breathed out a silent sigh, relieved she hadn't irritated Desmond as much as she had expected, but wondered why his mood seemed to change with each passing moment. She followed him outside and back down the street to the barricade where he barked some orders at Dani and Guardrail then grabbed Evie's baseball bat from Dani's grasp.

"Hey! I claimed that!" The purple-haired Dani shouted.

"Wasn't yours to claim. This belongs to Evie, unless you want to trade in one of your side arms for it," Desmond responded, handing the bat over to Evie.

"How about I fight her for it?" Dani smiled, showing her crooked, too large teeth.

"How about you fight me for it?" Desmond leaned in and quietly but angrily mused.

"Whatever, take the bat," Dani mumbled. As she stormed past, she shoulder-checked Evie, knocking her hard in the arm. "Des isn't going to be around to watch your back all the time."

Evie ignored the larger girl's taunt, Dani did outweigh Evie by a solid thirty pounds and had years of experience fighting that Evie did not. She would need to pick her battles with the girl carefully, if she had to battle her at all. Proud of herself for biting her tongue and taking the higher road, yet still somewhat irritated it had come to that, Evie turned her back to Dani. She began walking in Desmond's direction, so that they might be on their way and begin their mission of finding insulin for his ailing uncle.

Quick footsteps behind her should've given Evie an idea of what was about to take place, but instead the hard kick to the back of her knees blindsided her before she fell forward to the ground. Landing on her knees, Evie felt a sharp pain and knew she probably had a new hole in her ragged jeans as well as skinned knees to boot. She managed to catch herself with her hands before her face hit, and her hands were a bit skinned as well.

"Ain't nuthin' changed. Be tripping nerds just like in high school," Dani proclaimed.

Evie slowly regained her composure and stood to her feet. She took a breath, as well as a moment to consider what she was about to say and smiled as she did.

"You're right, Dani. Very little has changed. You still have the social graces of an ape, and the face to match."

"Getting mouthy are ya? You think because you moved up north and you're a fancy Yankee bitch, you're better than all us now?"

"Dani, I knew I was better than you long before I ever moved and became a *fancy Yankee bitch.*"

Dani lunged forward, crowding Evie. She was a bit shorter than Evie, but she rose to meet her eye to eye. She stared unblinking at Evie and with her middle finger and thumb, thumped Evie in the forehead.

"What are ya gonna do now?" Dani quipped.

When Evie had no answer, Dani replied, "I didn't think so."

As Dani turned to walk away, without thinking her actions through, Evie drew the bat back and swiftly swung it aiming at the backs of Dani's knees knocking her to the ground very similar to how Evie had just fallen. Evie's blood seemed to run hot and she could hear her heartbeat in her ears as she realized what she had done. As her mind raced, she knew the next few moments would dictate how the rest of her dealings with Dani would transpire. If she backed down now, the girl would run all over her. If she fought, she'd probably get hurt. Then again, Desmond had seemed to want to stick up for her. Maybe he would lend a hand.

Dani scrambled to get up, falling down once, but fumbling to her feet in a final push from the ground. Her eyes narrowed and Evie noticed her fists clinched giving Evie just enough notice before the girl pounced in her direction like a mad bull.

Evie wildly swung the bat as Dani neared causing the angered girl to dodge and throw herself back.

"You're brave with that bat, but I'm still going to kick your ass!" Dani howled.

In what Evie quickly realized was a horrible judgment call, she threw the bat to the ground and held up her fists, ready to take on the biker chick hand to hand. As the bat rolled across the ground, Evie noticed that horrible uneven smile of Dani's as she lurched forward.

A throbbing pain exploded across Evie's face as Dani's quick punch landed square on Evie's eye. She blinked hard, opened her eyes in just enough time to see another fist coming at her face. With little time to react, Evie dodged, but Dani still managed to land a solid punch on Evie's ear. Another burst of pain spread from the side of her face to her jaw and an odd ringing sound filled her head.

Losing her balance, Evie toppled to the ground and grabbed her ear, taking inventory of her injuries. Her quick triage assessment led her to believe that no real damage had been done, but surprisingly hurt like hell. As many of the superficial wounds from bar fights she had treated during her rounds as a medical student, she never imagined it would actually be as painful as it was.

Dani stood over Evie, grinning as though she had easily enough proven her point. Evie had hoped if she stuck up for herself that the girl would back down, but she had been horribly wrong.

"You know how to pick 'em, Des. This one's got no use. I can't believe she's lived this long."

A rage Evie wasn't even aware she possessed rose to the surface. The pain subsided and anger took its place. The mush-mouthed, illiterate slut would pay for questioning Evie's worth or ability to survive. She had fought to stay alive for months, and no biker tramp would dismiss that. In a flash, Evie braced herself and kicked Dani in the leg with all her might, knocking her down.

THE LAST ONES

Evie's initial reaction was to wonder if she had broken one of the small bones in the girl's leg, but her medical reflex disappeared when she caught sight of Dani's angered face. Quickly Evie jumped atop Dani and began hitting with one fist, then the other in quick succession. Raised voices behind Evie muted into a dull roar that was unintelligible as she punched Dani over and over.

Evie became confused when she could no longer reach Dani's face. She seemed to be levitating from the ground away from her opponent, until she noticed the two arms on each side of her had lifted her and pulled her away. Desmond, and another Soldier of Chaos that she only knew as Jug, an older man around her uncle's age, held each of her arms.

Dani's face was bloody. She would no doubt have two black eyes, and Evie hoped a broken nose. All that hitting surely had done some damage beyond just some bruising. Guardrail lifted his girlfriend to her feet, but held her back as she thrust herself forward in one last attempt to get at Evie.

"Ugly bitch blind-sided me!" Dani wailed.

"Me ugly? It may be the apocalypse but I know there are still mirrors. Try looking in one, you purple-haired skank!" Evie shouted.

Dani wrestled to free herself of Guardrail's hold to no avail, finally giving in. As all the fight seemingly left her body, Guardrail held Dani underneath her arms and her body went limp.

"That's enough. This will end here and now or the next punches thrown at you two will be coming from my fists. We clear?" Desmond roared.

Dani nodded her head, but Evie glared at the man through her blurred vision as she gritted her teeth. Evie's family would never condone a man being violent with a woman, and Evie had no intention of letting any person, woman, man or biker rough her up. She would take them all down if necessary.

"You can wipe that look off your face. This ain't high school anymore, Evie. I make the rules," Desmond asserted. He kept his grip around her forearm, even after Dani was drug away and Jug released her other arm. "Come on, we have things to do."

"And I should still help you, why?" Evie questioned.

"Because if you don't I'll throw you and your family out of here tonight. You want to try to find shelter in the dark with two old ladies and a gimp uncle?"

For once, Evie thought about her next words before she spoke. She did not want her actions to be the reason her family perished. Although she wanted to kill every last one of the people there in their sleep, she had little recourse.

"Let's get something straight, come daybreak, my family and I are leaving with our weapons. I'm not helping you for any other reason than at this moment I don't have a choice."

"I never thought you would for any other reason," Des retorted.

"Well, you should have. A couple hours ago, I was helping your uncle and you because it was the right thing to do and I thought you might still be a decent person. I was horribly wrong," Evie said. Instantly she regretted her honesty. She wanted to wound him with her words and make him feel the same pain that she felt when Dani punched her, but nothing she had said came out as malicious as she had intended.

Expecting a quick insult or even a laugh, Evie was surprised at Desmond's reaction. His face fell, and he began to speak, but stopped himself. For that moment, Evie thought she saw some real emotion, but as quickly as that hurt look had shown across his face, it was gone.

CHAPTER EIGHT

The massive search through the Health Department patient records had yielded a few results. She had located the home addresses of seven diabetics who lived a reasonable distance from the blockade and used insulin. Most of the patients she'd found had Type 2 Diabetes and required only medication in pill form. If Priest had been anyone else in the world, he would've garnered Evie's pity for having such a grueling condition, especially in the situation the world was currently in. Maintenance for a person with insulin-dependent diabetes would prove to be nearly impossible. He would constantly have to be looking for blood glucose test strips, insulin, needles, lancets to poke his fingers and other supplies. Not to mention he would always need to keep some form of glucose handy in case his blood sugar bottomed out, and food was at times, scarce.

Evie had come across a few diabetics in her rounds. Many practiced good maintenance and remained healthy, but on the occasion she ran into a non-compliant patient, her heart went out, because the complications were so devastating. Nerve damage, kidney damage, heart disease, the list went on. Some of the patients had even gone blind and one had needed a leg amputated. Priest remaining days would be difficult at best.

"Let's try the house on Olive first. It's only a couple blocks away," Desmond suggested.

Evie dutifully followed behind, saying nothing.

"I was thinking we would head on over to the other house on Dogtown Road afterwards, then if we haven't found anything, try the one on by the Elementary school," Desmond added.

Evie continued to follow noiselessly.

"Most of these areas have been cleared out, but I still thought it was too dangerous to take the bike with all the noise. We still have the occasional straggler shamble up to the barricade from time to time. I hope you don't mind all this walking."

Moments passed without Evie ever speaking a word.

"We need to be careful when we enter the houses. We've been traveling through the streets getting supplies on a daily basis, and we kill any of the zombies on the streets, but there may be some left in the houses we go in. Cool?"

When Evie refused to answer yet again, Desmond stopped so suddenly, Evie almost ran into him. He spun around, grabbed her hard by the shoulders and squeezed.

"What is your problem?" He demanded.

"Seriously?" Evie calmly asked.

Desmond relaxed his grip a bit, his face becoming a mixture of anger and confusion.

"You hit women. You threaten women. You are kind to me one moment, the next you tell me you will throw my family and me out and let us die. You let Dani humiliate me without saying a word, and all I've done is try to help you," Evie paused as her voice began to rise in volume. "What you don't seem to understand is, you people act so tough, but threatening women, that just shows how weak you all truly are. I will say this to you once, and only once. You threaten me again, you or anyone else raises a hand to me, including your uncle, I will kill you."

Evie jerked her shoulders lose and stepped away from Desmond. She tightened her grip on the baseball bat and looked into his eyes as menacingly as she could.

"You almost make me believe you could," Desmond answered.

"Oh, I could, and I will. Don't confuse me with those weak-minded sluts that you keep around."

"Wouldn't dream of it," Des smirked as he spoke.

***

If he thought he liked her before, Desmond knew, he was full-blown in love with her now. *Hard to believe a beautiful woman threatening to kill a man could have that effect, yet it certainly did,* he thought. He tried to act dismissive toward her intimidations, but in fact, Desmond did believe her.

The only person he had ever seen his uncle back down to was a woman, Desmond's very own mother. She was much like Evie, smart, beautiful and kind. She also had that same spunk. He was certain his mother would've loved Evie.

Evie was so similar to how he remembered her. She was spunky, smart, kind and somehow so very serious at times. He'd never known another woman quite like his mother, until now. Some of his brother's old ladies were nice enough, but even the best of them weren't in the same caliber as Evie and his mom. He could never imagine Evie in all her perfection wanting to be some biker old lady, but that was part of what made him like her. Plus she was beautiful.

Maybe he'd been looking at everything the wrong way. He had come up with every excuse he could think of to reason why he and Evie could never be together. However, there was a very influential factor that he hadn't fully considered. Competition was scarce. The men who remained in town with his club were mostly of inappropriate age, the few who weren't had even less chance than he did.

Des wasn't one to toot his own horn, but when it came to him and Guardrail, he knew he was the obvious choice. Sure, they had been best friends for years, but he had to admit, the boy was a little dense. Not to mention he had Dani to keep him entertained. *Could he really have half a chance with Evie?* Yes, he decided it was in the realm of possibility. He just needed to win her over and stop flying off the handle out of frustration. He'd never actually liked a woman like this.

"Desmond!" Evie loudly whispered.

"What is it, woman?" Desmond answered sharply as he was jerked back to reality from his thoughts. he shut his eyes and sighed, he had just snapped at her again.

"You're about to walk past the house. What is wrong with you?" Evie scornfully questioned.

"I'm sorry. I had some things on my mind."

"Why don't you and your deep thoughts guard the porch and watch out for any rotters? I'll go check the fridge," she offered.

"Hell no, I'm not letting you walk in there by yourself. Wait, what did you call them?" He asked.

"Rotters?" Evie responded, then began giggling as she realized how silly the term sounded out loud.

"I like it. Rotters," Desmond laughed.

"Fine, you go in. Do you know what you're looking for?" Evie asked.

"Of course, I lived with the man for years. I'll be right back."

Desmond tested the doorknob and it turned. Other than the door squeaking a bit as he pushed it open, Desmond slipped silently inside the house. Evie sat on the front porch carefully watching both directions of the street, back and forth. It was quiet.

She could hear Desmond rummaging around inside and was curious if he had found any insulin. If the homeowners had fled the area, they would've taken it with them. If he found it, most likely that meant the residents of the cute little sage green sided house were deceased. The world had become quite a depressing place.

A rustling noise in the shrubs to the side of the house alerted Evie to the presence of something. It was moving in her direction.

She peeped through the picture window of the home to see Desmond's flashlight's glow shining in what she imagined was the kitchen and the light sounds of glass clinging and being moved. Evie dared not shout for Desmond, but knew a rotter would be much easier to handle with the help of her much stronger companion, but she could easily handle a single one by herself.

Instead of waiting, Evie tiptoed down the porch and slinked around the corner of the house to where the noise had originated. The bushes were somewhat small and had probably once been neatly trimmed, a few wild sprigs here and there were really all that made them appear unruly. She convinced herself that no rotter could've hidden within, until she considered the possibility of it being very small. A child could hide there.

Evie was sickened by the thought. She hadn't come across any afflicted children. Of course, children could be exposed just as adults. Why she hadn't considered that, she was unsure. She hoped her luck would continue and she wouldn't stumble upon one. The idea of braining a child, zombie or not, was revolting.

Warily, Evie squatted to the ground and peeped under the row of bushes. As she scanned the ground for something that could be making the noise, she imagined finding the tiny feet of a toddler. Her stomach lurched at the thought, yet she clinched up on her bat in preparation. Fortunately, nothing was to be seen. Only a garden hose and spigot hid behind the hedge, but an old gray cat darted across the yard, pulling Evie's attention to the back of the house.

"Evie! Evie!" Desmond screamed from the porch.

Evie raced to the front porch to find Desmond grasping several bottles of insulin, yet extremely agitated.

"Where the hell were you?" He demanded.

"I heard something. I was checking it out just on this side of the house," Evie hissed.

"Do not wander off without me. Ever. You get me?" Desmond commanded with a finger pointed in her face.

"Do not expect me to take orders. I go where I want and do what I want, and right now I've had enough of you."

Evie stormed off in the direction of the safely barricaded area of town.

***

"Evie?" Desmond whispered.

"Evie?" He asked again.

Evie paused, holding her index finger to her lips. She motioned for him to keep quiet, and she began a careful check of the area.

Evie roughly grabbed Desmond by his shirttail and yanked him alongside her in a small alcove between two brick buildings. She squeezed in close to him, making sure any view of them was completely hidden from the street.

"Well, hello there," Desmond purred.

A clanking noise interrupted Evie's response, and Desmond drew his gun from a side holster.

He peeped around the building and pulled another handgun from the back of his pants and handed it to Evie.

"Too loud," she whispered.

"Too many," Desmond urged.

Evie peered around the corner to find a group of six rotters cresting over the hill near the old courthouse building. She ducked her head back into the small nook where she and Desmond were now trapped.

"Think you can handle three?" He asked.

Evie stuck her head around the corner once again to confirm the numbers. All six were quickly advancing toward the couple's hiding spot.

"Can you?" Evie fumed in her most sarcastic tone.

With no regard to his answer, Evie emerged from the nook with only her baseball bat. With an athletic stance she had no idea she possessed, Evie hastened toward the first of the herd with her club drawn and readied to swing.

A thud resounded through the bat more than any actual noise, and Evie's hands took the hard recoil of the swing that knocked the rotter to the ground. She had hit him square in the temple and he no longer moved or even twitched.

Sidestepping to the next in line, Evie cleaved the bat downward in a chopping motion and toppled the next zombie, a small, older woman still dressed in her dirtied white nightgown. Unlike the first, she flailed and reached at Evie from her prone position on the ground. Evie gave another hard swing to the back of her neck and the rotter stilled.

Moving on to the next, Evie became wary that the remaining four were in close proximity and might gang up on her. The zombies were somewhat easy to handle one at a time, but contending with multiple rotters proved to be not only difficult but deadly. One bite, and it was over.

Evie juked to the far left, and the group began to follow, one leading with the other three trailing several feet behind. Evie bashed him in the temple with all her might, just as she had the first one, and watched him fall and become motionless.

She began to size up the last three when Desmond pushed her aside and shot the remaining rotters with superb accuracy, giving each one bullet to the forehead.

Evie opened her mouth to chastise Des for using the loud firearm, but before she could speak, she noticed what he had obviously already had seen. Even more were cresting over the hill. Around a dozen were hastening toward the gunshot, straight for them.

"Take the left side. I'll go right," Evie directed.

Des flashed a questioning look for only moment, then nodded before he began sprinting up the hill shooting every zombie on his side of the street, and a few on hers.

Evie made quick work of the dead who were in her path. Her hands stung each time her bat connected with a rotter's head, but she made certain to put enough force behind each blow to take them out in one swing. There were so many, with more coming, she had no time to focus on any one zombie without another creeping within biting distance.

Checking the other side of the street for Des, she saw him stabbing the rotters with a long hunting knife, similar to hers. Either he was afraid of drawing more out with the noise, or more likely, he had run out of ammunition.

Evie slowed as she waited for Desmond to catch up. The street was mostly quiet and the remaining road to the barricade was clear.

As they neared the biker's stronghold, Evie noticed a familiar figure standing atop a semi truck, rifle pointed in her direction. Waving her arms and sucking in hard to catch her breath, Evie yelled.

"Uncle Del!"

"I see ya, Hot Rod! Get on in here!" He squawked with his rifle still lined up as Evie ran toward the wall of trucks and tires, which fashioned the wall to the encampment.

A shot rang out and Evie realized Uncle Del had fired at something closely trailing her. She spun to see a solo rotter lying on the ground where one hadn't been seconds earlier. It must've been hot on her heels. All the exertion had left her winded and gasping for air so loudly she hadn't heard it.

Desmond began climbing the debris they had used to close off the street and build the blockade. He vaulted himself atop the bed of a pickup truck full of tractor tires, and scurried to the roof, offering Evie a hand. She flung her bat up in the truck, then taking Desmond's hand, climbed to join him. He easily ascended each obstacle jumping from one hunk of metal to another as sure-footed as a mountain goat. With every few steps, he would reach behind and offer a hand to Evie, who carefully watched each step, almost tripping as she followed behind.

When they reached the top and joined Delmont, he was laughing and sharing a drink from a mason jar with Jug, the burly biker who was close in age and size.

"Damn fine shooting, Del," Jug slapped Evie's uncle on the shoulder and retrieved the mason jar from his grasp.

"You want the next one?" Del asked.

Jug aimed with one hand and fired accurately, killing another one.

"Damn fine shooting and shine, Jug!" Del howled. "Hey Hot Rod, did I ever tell you that Jug here and I were stationed together in boot camp?"

"No," Evie answered, and seemed to understand the sudden bond between the two men wasn't sudden at all.

"Your Uncle Del here was quite the character. He wouldn't listen to no one or nothin'. I bet a did a blue million push-ups because this here ole boy couldn't learn to take an order!" Jug chortled.

"Don't you be giving my niece any wrong ideas, now!" Del laughed.

"As much as I'd love to stay and hear more about my uncle's illustrious military career that I seemed to have gotten all wrong, I really need to get these supplies back to the Health Department. Is Mom and Granny okay?" Evie asked.

"Yeah, yeah, they visited with Hazel and headed back to the house about an hour ago," Del replied.

Evie hugged her uncle and gave him a quick peck on the cheek. He had after all saved her with his impeccable shooting. Evie wondered how much moonshine he had drank though. She had never known Uncle Delmont to ever have even a sip of liquor, yet he seemed to be swigging the moonshine and shooting just fine. *Maybe there was a whole different side to her uncle,* Evie thought.

She shook the thought from her head, and carefully began her descent to the ground and other side of the makeshift bulwark. Desmond followed closely behind.

"Ev?" Desmond croaked.

"Yeah?"

"So the insulin I found tonight says Novolog. My uncle has been using one called Humalog. Will that work?" He asked.

"Yes, they are both fast-acting insulin. You really need to find a long-acting insulin too. It will be called Lantus or Levemir. He needs that as well and quickly."

"See, we need you here. None of us know anything about how to help each other when we are sick or hurt, plus I've seen a whole new side to you. You're a zombie-killing machine, girl. I hope you will stay," Desmond's tone was very persuasive, but not in his usual demanding way.

"I'll get back to you on that. Let's get this to your uncle," Evie suggested.

CHAPTER NINE

Evie rejoined her mother and grandmother in their new shelter in just enough time to fill them in on the evening's events, withholding the part about her catfight with Dani, of course. She then watched them excitedly get ready to go to work at Hazel's café just before dawn. Evie hadn't considered that Retta and Birdie were just as bored as she. The two women seemed thrilled to have a purpose and eagerly discussed what they could cook the townspeople for breakfast. Evie smiled as the two women left and shut her eyes hoping for a few minutes of sleep before she needed to get up and find out what she, herself, would be scheduled to do for the day.

Just as she began to doze off, Uncle Del stumbled through the door waking her. Evie shut her eyes again, but the urgency for sleep had vanished and she reluctantly crawled from her mat and made her way to the front room of the building to find her uncle.

"How did it go last night?" Evie asked.

"We had a big time!" Del answered with a booming chortle.

"So you and Jug go way back, huh?" she questioned.

"Jug, he was always a rough customer, but he's a good man. Back in boot camp he and I got to be right good friends. Man's darn good with a rifle and a wrench."

Del had given the biker, Jug, one of his highest compliments. Evie knew how her uncle respected anyone who could take care of themselves as well as their own vehicles.

"So did you guys see much action last night?"

"The most excitement we seen all night was when you and that pretty boy come runnin' up with that gang of dead. I know you can take care of yourself, Hot Rod, but I ain't so sure about that boy. He may try to look all tough, but he's right smart girly with that shaggy hair," Uncle Del smirked and raised his eyebrows in question.

"What's that look for?" Evie defensively asked. She knew her uncle all too well.

"You ain't getting sweet on him, are ya?"

"Of course not!" Evie denied. "Why on Earth would you think that?"

"You're a pretty young girl, and there's a lack of eligible young men these days. I'm just sayin'. Now you keep in mind, you're sharp as a tack, you're tough and you've got everything going for ya. You ain't gotta settle for no thug."

"No worries, Uncle Del. I'm not planning on any white dresses and picket fences anytime soon," Evie joked.

Uncle Del reached out and motioned for Evie to come to him and gave her a big, fatherly hug. He kissed her on her forehead.

"I just want you to be happy. I know it's gonna be a hard way to go here these days, but it don't mean you can stop living. I had forgotten myself what fun a man can have just from keepin' good company until last night. You're mama and granny are excited to be here too. I just want you to find some happiness."

"Thanks. I'll try," Evie promised.

Del released the girl and began walking toward the back of the building when he stopped abruptly and turned around, pausing.

"Something else?" Evie asked.

"Yeah. I done heard about what happened yesterday. You better stay clear of that ole purple headed gal," Del beamed.

"Why are you smiling?" Evie asked.

"Whooped her, did ya?"

"She had it coming," Evie mumbled through gritted teeth remembering the event.

"You know what I always said. Don't be a bully, but if someone starts something with ya, you better finish it. Good job, Hot Rod," Del, still beaming, turned his back and walked out.

Evie was almost sure she could hear the man actually giggling in the back room.

***

Evie had paced the floor, attempted to brush out her hair and wash her face. She was out of things to do and found herself staring out the window watching as the town came to life and people began heading over to

Hazel's diner. When she saw Desmond cross the street and walk inside, Evie leaned down, took a quick whiff under her arms and headed toward the café herself.

It occurred to her as she followed others in that maybe her uncle had noticed something. Maybe she did have a little crush on Des. He was sort of ridiculously handsome for a guy who hadn't showered regularly in months or had a haircut. All considered, he was as her uncle had put it... pretty. Des was in great shape, she hadn't realized how much so until she had seen him fight through the horde, which was impressive in itself. Not to mention those piercing blue eyes. At times he could be almost charming. Of course most of the time, he was a giant butthead. Evie shook her head in an effort to dismiss the thought of him from her mind as she opened the door and entered the restaurant.

The place was filled and Evie looked around for a seat. The bar stools had been moved and set up around the edges of the room so that it was turned into a cafeteria-style buffet along the counter. Evie caught sight of her mother and grandmother quickly scooping out food to each person's plate as they made their way down the line.

Evie took her place in the back and within minutes was getting her portion of breakfast; white beans, a small piece of egg and half an apple. Under normal conditions, the meal would have been something worthy of a complaint for the fine home cooking of Hazel's diner, but under the circumstances, Evie was grateful to be eating.

Retta and Birdie were all smiles as they spoke to each person saying hello and making small talk as the line dwindled and everyone took a seat. Evie scanned the room and finally found an empty barstool in the corner. She carefully sat atop the chair and began to eat the rationed meal when suddenly the entire diner quieted to the point you could hear a pin drop. Priest stood at the front of the room with his arms crossed, next to him was Desmond holding a sheet of paper.

"Today is Wednesday, September 28. Jobs are as follows," Desmond read. "Guardrail, Dulane and Boots are on supply run. We're going to focus on houses around Mayfield Highway today. Hazel has made a list of items that she needs here in the kitchen, so be on the lookout for these and of course anything else that might be edible or useful," Desmond instructed and handed a ragged map with lots of marked off areas, as well as another piece of paper to Guardrail.

"Clean up crews – with new residents coming in, we are hoping to extend our boundaries up Main Street toward the flower shop. The last couple buildings before the barricade need to be cleaned out and set up with any additional blankets, cots or mattresses we have come by. Also, be sure to check the fences when you're done and report back any problems. Today is a pretty light day for you guys."

With Desmond's orders, a handful of people who had finished their meals stood and exited the restaurant. Evie assumed them to be the ones he had referred to as the clean up crew who were mostly older men and women and a couple young teens.

"Patrol from the north barricade is Chicken and Charlie Nunn."

Chicken, a gargantuan biker who stood around six and a half feet tall and easily weighing three hundred pounds stood, as did a little old man, Evie determined to be Charlie. The two headed toward the door.

"South barricade patrol will be Evie Stone and Dani Krenshaw."

Evie's mouth dropped as she stared at Des. *What was he thinking! She couldn't be put on duty with that ratchet skank of Guardrail's!*

Dani, bruised and badly beaten from the day before, rose and slammed her chair into the table. Clearly, she was just as unhappy as Evie about the assignment. Dani pushed her way through the diner and flung the door open, loudly rattling the bells hanging from the handle.

"Those of you I didn't give assignments to will be on patrols tonight. I'll post the schedule on the board," Desmond motioned to the corkboard by the jukebox as he finished.

Evie quickly dropped her plate in a plastic bussing container as she made a path to Desmond.

"I can't work with her," Evie avowed.

"You're going to have to. Everyone here has to work and get along," Des insisted.

"Just last night you told me to stay clear of her!"

"I had some time to think and it'd be best if the two of you got this out of your systems and worked it all out."

"You mean you want us to fight again?" Evie asked incredulously.

"No, if you two fight again, I warned you that I would intervene, and neither of you will like that," Desmond's tone lowered and the look in his eyes angered Evie.

"You think you can be so threatening and scare people into doing whatever whim you have. You don't scare me. Trust me on this, you are better off on *my* good side than my bad, Desmond Young," Evie turned, flipping her hair and stomped away. As she walked through the door she heard Priest laugh and call Desmond a sissy.

Evie swallowed hard, straightened her posture and headed toward the south barricade. It had been the one she and her family had entered when they arrived the previous day. Dani had been on duty the day before with Guardrail. Evie wondered if jobs were always mixed up or if she'd be stuck with Dani every day. She wouldn't take that, she'd leave before she suffered that skank's ignorance on a daily basis.

Before she started her duty, Evie veered across the street to her family's new residence and grabbed her baseball bat that she had left just inside the door. She wasn't sure if she would be given another weapon, and dared not show up without something. She was thankful Des hadn't remembered to confiscate it after the insulin run.

By the time Evie got there, Dani was already perched atop the barricade, lounging in a lawn chair with a shotgun rested across her lap. Evie carefully climbed around her and sat as far from the girl as she could, which still allowed her a line of vision down the street and across the small creek. The platform was only about ten foot across, forcing Evie to sit entirely too close to the shotgun wielding skeezer. Minutes passed and turned to almost an hour before either of them spoke.

"Evie Stone," Dani mocked. "You know we used to call you Heavy Stone back in middle school when you were fat."

"I was never fat, you just started doing meth back then and looked like a skinny crackhead," Evie retorted.

Dani laughed. "I didn't do meth back then, and I guess I was the only one who called you that. But everyone did call you nerd and geek," she snarled.

"Instead of Dani Krenshaw, everyone called you Dani Creepshow," Evie smiled devilishly as she spoke.

"No, they didn't!" Dani angrily argued.

"Yeah, actually they did."

"Well, screw 'em all. They're all dead now, aren't they?" Dani reasoned.

"You can find a bright point to anything, can't ya?" Evie sarcastically asked.

"Kids are mean," Dani said.

"You were mean. You *are* mean," Evie replied.

"Not really. Just stick up for myself," Dani said then paused with a questioning look. "Tell me something. Truth, okay?"

"What do you want to know?" Evie asked.

"You hot for Des?"

"What? Of course not!" Evie answered.

"Yeah, I figured. You still think you're too good for him."

"I never said that. He's just not my type."

"You mean you're too good for him?" Dani persisted.

"I'm too good to be with someone who hits women, yes," Evie answered.

"He's not usually like that. It's your fault. You've got him acting all stupid."

"How is him being abusive my fault?" Evie asked.

"Because for some reason I think he likes you. I mean, it's not like there's a ton of single chicks around, so he's obviously desperate, so don't get all big-headed about it."

"I'm not sure why it matters to you, but here's the truth. He treats me like crap. He doesn't like me like that, or any other way. In fact, I'm pretty sure the only reason I'm even here is because I can fix any of you idiots up when you hurt yourselves, so get over it. I'm not going to be some competition for 'Biker Old Lady of the Year.'"

Dani laughed.

"I'll leave you alone as long as you leave him alone," Dani declared as she gazed down the street and pointed. "Head's up, nerd."

A zombie slowly walked between the buildings and began shambling in the direction of the barricade.

"I haven't seen a straggler like that just walk up in forever. Lucky day!" Dani exclaimed and aimed her shotgun.

"Wait!" Evie whispered, "She looks so familiar."

The two girls strained as the zombie staggered closer until it was only yards away from the barricade. The female rotter's hair was big and messy, and somehow a thick line of eyeliner had managed to remain on her lids.

"Oh my gosh, that's Nichole Martin!" Evie shouted.

"Right! I remember her. I couldn't stand her in school," Dani retorted.

"She tried to steal my boyfriend once," Evie recalled.

"You may be a nerd, but she was a total fat pig. She actually looks way better as a zombie."

Evie cocked her head in a contemplative look then glanced back up at Dani.

"You know, she does," Evie agreed.

The two women began cackling until the creature that used to be Nichole made it to the barricade and started scratching and reaching toward them.

"Give me a twinkie and your boyfriend, Heavy Stone," Dani mocked in a groaning voice as the rotter clawed at the barricade.

Dani aimed the shotgun, but before she fired, Evie raised her hand in a halting motion and leaned over the barricade smacking Nichole atop her head with her baseball bat cracking it open like a putrid melon.

"Felt good, didn't it?" Dani asked.

"Actually yeah, kind of did!"

"I'll crack your skull like that if you screw with Desmond's head anymore though."

"And here I thought we were becoming friends," Evie rolled her eyes, no longer feeling very threatened by the odd girl.

CHAPTER TEN

That afternoon, two bikers, Swifty and Scoop, came to relieve Dani and Evie of their duties. The day had been relatively uneventful, short of the excitement of bashing a high school nemesis in the head. Evie wasn't quite ready to head back to her makeshift home so she made her way to the old Health Department. If Hazel was able to make lists for the supply runs, maybe they would allow her to do the same and the people who went outside of the barricade could look for medical necessities as well, Evie reasoned.

Unsure whether to just walk in or not, Evie gently knocked on the glass of the door. No one answered, so she knocked again. A few seconds later, a shirtless, heavily tattooed Priest was standing at the door, clearly upset with his visitor.

"What do you want?" He growled.

"I thought I could check out the supplies here and maybe make a list of things we could use," Evie answered.

"Yeah, that's not a bad idea. Come on," Priest grumbled as he threw the door open.

Evie reluctantly entered, realizing now she was alone with the most dangerous man in town. She began to regret her decision to help.

"I don't want you to get the wrong idea, little girl," Priest started and hesitantly began again, "but I want to thank you for helping me yesterday."

"What am I to get the wrong idea about?" Evie asked.

"That I like you. Because I don't," he answered.

"Well, glad you made that clear. I was starting to think you were my new BFF," Evie quipped.

Priest grabbed Evie and forcibly spun her to meet his gaze.

"You need to understand something. There's no one here to protect you if you make me mad. The second I find you more trouble than useful, I'll make you go away."

Evie was terrified of the man, but she did all she could to hide that fact.

"I'm sorry, did we somehow switch roles? You see, I thought I was the doctor who made sure you stayed alive. I'm unsure why you dislike me so much, but I've done nothing to deserve this treatment and you've done everything to deserve my anger."

"You just do your job and stay away from my nephew, understand?" Priest leaned in, staring into Evie's eyes with the most menacing look she'd ever seen.

Evie jerked her arm away from the biker and stormed out. She'd worry about supplies later, and she'd not set foot in that building again or help that psycho. The grizzled, sickly old man and Dani had both made threats against her to stay clear of Des, not to mention her uncle's warning. The one thing Evie hated more than anything was being told she couldn't do something, however, not getting too close to Desmond did at times seem like a good idea. Too bad she knew she wouldn't stay away.

Running through everything she'd wished she had said to Priest in her mind, Evie began noticing her fellow survivors were all quickly making their way back to Hazel's Diner. *It must be the dinner rush*, she thought. Although she'd hardly had anything to eat, she wasn't hungry. A fiery anger filled her belly and she was in no mood to be around others, especially those who wore those stupid leather jackets.

As she passed the diner, on her way back to her family's residence, Evie gazed through the windows of Hazel's and saw her mom and grandmother once again doling out portions of food to a line of people. They were smiling and chatting, unlike Evie had seen them in months. As much as she hated being in their new community, her family seemed to be flourishing. She'd so often thought about finding other survivors, making friends and having someone else to talk to besides her family. It seemed they needed that as well, and she dared not tell them how miserable she was and ruin their happiness.

***

It was far too early to sleep, and Evie found herself bored to tears. Her uncle had guard duty with Jug again that evening and Retta and Birdie were still at Hazel's cleaning up and prepping for the next day. Evie grabbed her baseball bat and was headed out the door when she heard the commotion.

From the other side of the barricade crying mingled with shouts grabbed Evie's attention and she began running toward the gate she had been posted at earlier that day. When Evie got there, Scoop, one of the bikers who had relieved her shift was opening the gate.

"Drop the gun, son," Swifty demanded, as the stranger was granted access.

To Evie's surprise, in wandered three adorable little blond girls, and trailing behind their father, Trevor Thomas.

"Evie! You're here?" Trevor asked seemingly shocked.

"You got any more weapons on ya, son?" Swifty asked.

"Evie, go get Priest or Des back here now," Scoop ordered.

Evie began jogging up the street following the biker's directions as she shouted behind, "Just do what they ask, Trevor, I'll be right back!"

Evie knew she'd find Priest in the Health Department, but she had no desire to see him, so she began searching out Desmond. Their safe zone only consisted of a few blocks, so she didn't have far to look. She began with Hazel's Diner.

Evie popped her head in the door, grabbing the attention of Hazel, who was cleaning tables.

"Miss Hazel, have you seen Des?"

"He left a bit ago. Try the blue house behind the Health Department," Hazel suggested.

Evie took off and began sprinting to the little house Hazel had referred to, which made good sense. She hadn't been sure exactly where Des stayed, but she should have figured it would've been close to his uncle's.

Evie smiled as she ran. Maybe things were looking up. Finally, she had someone in town she knew and liked. She and Trevor had always gotten along and reminiscing with him when she'd run into him while hunting had been the highlight of her return back home. Evie was almost skipping.

Taking two steps at a time, Evie pounced across the porch of the blue house and without even thinking of knocking. In her excitement, she flung open the screen door and let herself inside. To her surprise, Des wasn't alone, and even more surprising, was the awkward scenario to which she had now witnessed. Up against Des, was Dani kissing him.

Evie's abrupt entrance had interrupted them, and they both stared at her in what seemed to be as much disbelief as she.

"I'm so sorry. They told me to find you. There is someone at the south gate," Evie blurted in embarrassment.

Des pushed Dani away, narrowing his eyes as though he was angry at her, instead of Evie who had clearly been the one at fault for the interruption. Des grabbed Evie by the arm and pulled her outside, almost dragging her down the street.

"Let go of me!" Evie wailed, as she hit Des in the shoulder with all her might, but to no avail.

"That wasn't what you thought you saw," he heatedly explained.

"I saw nothing," Evie adamantly denied.

"I want to explain," Desmond's tone quieted, yet seemed just as sharp as before.

"There is no need. I understand clearly. Whatever is going on is none of my business, and I have no intention of repeating what I saw to Guardrail, or anyone else for that matter. You have no need to worry. You can get with whatever you want."

"It isn't like that."

"I don't care what it's like," Evie lied. "Trevor Thomas is at the gate with his children and they need you there. We need to go."

Desmond shook his head and began walking again. Evie followed closely behind. Moments later, Desmond stopped unexpectedly and Evie smacked into his back and began to fall until Des grabbed her arm and pulled her to him.

"Didn't you date Trevor?" Desmond roared.

"Yeah, like eight years ago before he had kids. Why?" Evie asked.

Without an answer Desmond began walking again but with an urgency he hadn't had. As they arrived at the south gate, they found Scoop, Swifty and Trevor all laughing, the latter holding two of his girls, who were no longer crying, on each hip.

"So, you looking for refuge?" Des hissed.

"Yeah, man. Good to see you! We used to go to school together, right?" Trevor asked.

"How many you got?" Desmond questioned.

"You mean how many people? It's just us, me and my three girls," Trevor answered.

"Where's your wife?"

"She is visiting family out of state," Trevor sorrowfully replied.

"Since the outbreak, you mean, she's been gone since the beginning?"

"Yeah."

Desmond looked to Evie, sucked his teeth then stared back at Trevor.

"I don't think we have a place for you here."

"Are you insane? You can't turn him and three small children away this time of day! They will be killed out there!" Evie protested.

"They can stay tonight, but need to make their way somewhere else tomorrow," Des dictated and turned on his heel to leave.

Evie glanced at Trevor to find a shocked expression. She immediately began chasing Des down the street. Evie grabbed his arm and Desmond jerked it away.

"You can't turn them away!" She yelled.

"I have more people to think about than your ex-boyfriend and his rugrats. I have dozens of people who we can barely feed now as it is. I can't take on any more."

"Really? Is it because you're thinking of the others or are you thinking of yourself? Maybe you just don't want anyone as young, good-looking and capable here," Evie contended.

"Keep it up and you'll be out on your ass with him," Desmond growled as he stormed off.

Evie had no idea what to tell Trevor and his three little girls, but she knew there was no way she would let a bunch of bikers exile them from the only safety that existed.

CHAPTER ELEVEN

Evie grinned from ear to ear as three beautiful little girls raced to be the first to present her with dandelions they had picked. The small yard behind the old gift shop where Evie and her family resided was overrun with the yellow weeds, but it was a quiet and peaceful place, just across the fence from a small stream that ran through town.

Trevor reminded his girls to play quietly, but for three small children all under the age of six, Evie found them to be wonderfully behaved. They quietly giggled as they placed the flowers in Evie's hair and lined them up around where she sat.

"Daddy, look she's a princess," one whispered.

"She always was a princess," Trevor joked, knowing his children wouldn't understand.

Evie knocked him in the shoulder for the remark and the girls laughed, then began playing again.

"We ran out of food. The girls are too thin and I couldn't keep trying to feed them scraps of squirrel for much longer. I don't know what we are going to do," Trevor confided.

"I'll figure something out," Evie promised.

"You gonna take on a bunch of bikers?" Trevor laughed.

"If I have to," Evie answered.

"Evie, you can't risk yourself and your family to help us. Don't do anything. Maybe Desmond will change his mind. I know I'm asking a lot for them to help me and three little girls who can't really contribute."

Evie suddenly had an idea. Maybe Desmond's mind was made up, but he couldn't ignore the wishes of his fellow club members. She'd work on them.

"I've got an idea. You guys just chill and I'll be back."

Evie rushed around the building and made haste to the barricade closest to her giftshop home. Swifty and Scoop were lounging atop the barricade of metal rubbish stacked next to the fencing as they joked and watched the streets beyond the gate.

"How you guys doing up there?" Evie asked as innocent and pleasantly as she could muster.

"What's up, Doc?" Swifty hollered, as Scoop laughed.

Evie began climbing the stacks of pallets and junk until she sat between the two men.

"So Swifty," Evie began. "You have a little boy, right? How old is he?"

"Remmy is nine, and Win's seven," Swifty beamed.

"Remmy and Win? What unusal names. I like that.," Evie was sure to compliment the man and get him in the best mood possible.

"Well, they're short for Remington and Winchester," Swifty proudly announced.

"Scoop, you have a boy as well, don't you?" Evie queried. She was certain she had seen him with a teenager that looked exactly like him.

"I sure do! Noodle's going on sixteen. He works on the clean up crew, but really he fixes the fences mostly. Des and Priest are planning on having him do supply runs here before too long. The boy is a fine aim," Scoop noted.

"Wow, that's awesome. Sounds like you guys have some fine children you've raised," Evie stated, unwilling to comment on the name of Scoop's child. She was unsure how to compliment the choice of calling his son 'Noodle' and hoped it was a nickname and not what was actually on his birth certificate.

"What's the questions for, Doc?" Swifty finally asked.

"Well, I was just thinking, from a scientific standpoint, as a doctor and such, you know…"

"What?" Scoop questioned when Evie paused.

"Well, it's just that, there's not many people left to propagate," she explained.

"Huh?" Scoop asked.

"You know, to make more people. Have children and all."

"Having kids in these times is hard," Swifty countered.

Evie determined she would have to appeal to the men on a level they understood instead of rambling on about saving humanity.

"Well, like I said, as a doctor and all, I understand how strong men like yourselves, and your boys will have needs," Evie choked down the need to vomit as she spoke.

"Huh?" Scoop again asked.

"You know, for women. Tough, alpha male types like yourselves, and your boys, well, you don't want a big sausage party left on Earth for them, now do you?" Evie joked.

The men began laughing hysterically.

"You're funny, Doc," Scoop declared when he caught his breath.

"I'm being totally serious," Evie smiled and gave them a knowing nod.

"Yeah, it's going to suck for them," Swifty agreed.

"Well, I was just thinking, that guy that showed up earlier, Trevor Thomas, he has three really pretty little girls. I mean, I know taking on more mouths to feed is tough, but someday your boys are going to want wives, or old ladies," Evie corrected. "It'd be a shame if we turned away their only hope at finding some," Evie urged.

It was clear that the wheels had begun to turn in Swifty's brain and she had made some headway in getting him on her side, but Scoop was still giving her a questioning look.

"What's the look for?" Evie asked.

"How old is them girls?"

"I think they are three, five and six," Evie answered.

"My boy is too old for them!"

Evie grinned devilishly. Once again she had a better argument than the men. "Now Scoop, how old are you?"

"Forty-one," the biker answered.

"And how old is your girlfriend?" Evie pursed her lips and raised her eyebrows.

"Twenty-two," Scoop declared. He then laughed, as it was obvious the light bulb above his head had flickered on. "Point taken, Doc."

"I'm sure you guys see right through me. I went to medical school to help people and I can't stand the idea of turning three little angels away to be killed when there are tough guys like you here to protect them, but I hope that you can see it's in your best interest or at least your boy's best interest to keep them around," Evie was laying the bull on thick, but it seemed to be working. "Anyway, it was just a thought. Of course, what happens around here is something that the guys in charge decide, so I just thought I'd plead their case to someone that mattered. When you guys vote on what to do, I know you'll make the right decision, whatever that is."

"Yeah, we always try to vote on what's best for the club, not just ourselves," Swifty informed her.

"Yeah, but we ain't had church or a vote in months, brother," Scoop reminded Swifty.

"If you guys don't vote, then how do you decide what to do?" Evie instigated.

"We voted back when this all started and held church for any problem that came up," Swifty answered, then explained further when he noticed Evie had a dumbfounded look on her face. "Church is our club meetings."

"Oh, I see. It's good that you guys can all agree on how to run things. I'm really glad to be in a place that has reasonable decision makers," Evie smiled. "Listen guys, I better get moving, I'm sure I'll be on watch duty in the morning, so I better get some rest. Have a good night!"

Evie quickly descended the barricade and could hardly contain her smile as she overheard the two men whisper back and forth catching a word here and there. The revolution had begun and she was feeling a little like a rabble-rouser. Evie's malcontent of biker gang politics could cause their downfall if she kept working her silver-tongued magic. She branded herself an insurgent to the Soldiers of Chaos, and more specifically Desmond Young's stupid rules, and would do all she could to pit them against each other until she not only got what she wanted, but helped everyone else in town gain back control. For now though, she would sit back and watch the seed grow.

CHAPTER TWELVE

Evie was starving when she woke. Although she had barely gotten any sleep due to the fact Trevor and his girls had shared the residence with her and her family and kept her up most of the night, she managed to quickly crawl from bed. Evie cleaned herself up, preparing herself for breakfast at Hazel's.

Retta and Birdie were already gone, but Uncle Del slept silently in the corner of the room. The smell of pancakes and maple syrup permeated her nose, but she was certain it was only a dream and not reality. All the meals were minimal to say the least, nothing like a giant stack of pancakes.

Since the plague had hit, Evie found herself dreaming more and more about food. Sometimes she would have a nightmare about Sheena, or some old friend or family member chasing her and clawing at doors and windows in an effort to eat her brains, but for the most part she dreamt of rich, decadent food. That alone was more disturbing than the zombies because when Evie awoke each morning, her belly growled and there was no Boston cream pie or Baked Alaska left anywhere in the world, she suspected.

Hastily, she made her way to the diner where she found all the usual suspects. Bikers, their old ladies, a few townspeople and Hazel alongside her mother and grandmother flitting about bringing out pans of food and clean plates.

Evie sat at her usual barstool in the back, waiting for the line to shorten before she got her breakfast. The place seemed a bit louder than usual, but Evie attributed that to the fact she had barely slept and was easily irritated.

The bells on Hazel's front door loudly rattled as the door flung wide. Desmond stalked through and aggressively made his way to the front of the room. Without hesitation he began reading off the days assignments. Evie waited in anticipation for her name called, but instead she heard a name she hadn't expected.

"Trevor Thomas, south barricade watch," Desmond barked.

He finished calling out all the duties for the day, but never mentioned Evie. When the majority of the restaurant's inhabitants began to disband and head toward their appointed jobs, Evie followed Desmond to the cafeteria line and filed in behind him.

"You didn't call my name."

"My bad, I guess I forgot to mention that you have a new job now," Desmond gave her a caustic smile.

"Okay, great, what's that?" Evie asked.

"Well, since you went behind my back and schemed to make sure that your boyfriend Trevor and those little snots of his could stay, I figure someone needs to watch them now."

"So I'm babysitting?" Evie asked.

"Every child that is too young to work here. Yes. We've always made due and scheduled couples so that someone could watch the kids, but since Trevor is a single dad, we now require a full-time babysitter, plus it will give all the other parents a break, you know," Desmond almost sounded fair and reasonable, other than the slightly amused and sarcastic tone hidden beneath his words. "So I'm moving you out of the gift shop and into the big house on the corner of Poplar Street."

"Thanks, Des. Grandma Birdie will love that. She used to have a friend who lived there."

"Oh, don't thank me. Your family is staying where they are. *You* are moving there, and that will be your full-time residence. We have parents who work every shift, so you will stay at that house and watch the kids twenty-four, seven, get me?"

"So let me get this straight, you're trying to punish me for doing the right thing and wanting to protect three innocent little girls?"

"No, no punishment, just a job that is needed now and well, since you took it upon yourself to force my hand by manipulating my club, you should have to step up and deal with the consequences of the actions."

"Yet you are giving me the biggest, nicest house all to myself? I no longer have to sit in the sun and do guard duty all day and deal with your girlfriend, Dani?" Evie spoke slowly and smiled with each word with the intention of irritating him. "I'll see if I can't get punished again. Maybe next time you'll give me Dr. Vogle's Mercedes to drive around."

Before Desmond could respond, Evie sat her plate down and left, which she knew would make him even madder than what she had just said to him alone. She was playing with fire, but she didn't care. Rage began to boil up in her. Her hands began to feel hot and shake. *How dare he give her some crap job like babysitting when she clearly was capable of doing so much more!*

Of course, she hadn't meant a word of what she'd said in the diner. The house on Poplar was super nice, but on the complete other side of town and her family. Plus, she didn't want to be stranded anywhere twenty-four hours a day and certainly not with children day in and out. Not that she minded kids, she had even considered she might have one or two of her own someday, but not all the ones in town. She hated noise, messes and was easily agitated. She wasn't the kind of woman who was cut out to manage a herd of children and she knew it. Apparently, so did Des.

***

Within hours, Evie had the pleasure of becoming ward to Swifty's ill-behaved, hyperactive little psychos and all three of Trevor's little girls. Swifty's boys pulled Trevor's little girl's hair, pinched them, stomped on their feet and then spat at them. The girl's incessantly cried, the boys relentlessly screamed and Evie wanted to do both.

"Please, Miss Evie, make the mean boys stop," Macy, Trevor's oldest, pleaded.

After three hours of agonizing bedlam, Evie's resolve had broken. She no longer cared to play peacemaker between the two factions, instead she decided to level the playing field.

"It's school time boys and girls," Evie shouted.

Just as Evie expected, the boys began screaming.

"School sucks! We don't need no school!" Winchester, Swifty's youngest shouted.

Evie snorted as she refrained from explaining to Winchester that with his lack of skills in grammar he did, in fact, need a lot of school.

"Well, if you don't think you need it, I guess you boys can go play upstairs," Evie relented.

The boys immediately ran up the stairs and the floor above echoed with random crashing and breaking sounds.

"Girls, sit down, we are going to have Anatomy class," Evie directed.

"What's atomy class, Miss Evie?" Maddie, Trevor's middle girl, asked.

"Anatomy is the parts of your body. In Anatomy class you will learn where you can kick and hit mean little boys to make them stop," Evie smiled warmly at the girls and began to impart some valuable lessons they would no doubt remember for some time.

CHAPTER THIRTEEN

Evie was exhausted after her first day. Trevor and Swifty had picked up their children and no one else had dropped off any more. Evie assumed that meant she was off-duty for a bit, and began to pick up the mess of broken knick-knacks the boys had demolished.

The home's pre-zombie plague inhabitant seemed to be quite the aficionado of porcelain figurines, most of which appeared to be capodimonte probably purchased from a home shopping network. Little pieces of demolished flowers and people littered the upstairs and Evie sighed loudly as she crouched on her hands and knees collecting the shattered pieces.

She let out a loud shriek when a shard jabbed her in the palm. A riotous laugh made Evie jerk and knock over an accent table full of more curios, which fell to the floor. She turned to find Des, laughing even harder than he had initially.

"Can I help you with something?" Evie blustered.

"How'd daycare go today?" He asked in a cheeky tone.

"Actually it went well," Evie lied.

"Looks like it!" Des mocked.

"I enjoyed myself with all those lovely children. This place just wasn't set up to be a daycare, too many breakables for the kids to play and knock over. I'll have it fixed up by tomorrow," Evie explained, hoping he was buying her ridiculous fabrication.

"So you enjoyed yourself?" Desmond asked in seeming disbelief.

"Very much so. I just love working with kids. You know, I never realized how much pleasure one could derive from spending all day with such curious and interesting little people. We even learned a few things. I actually think I would've made an awesome teacher," Evie's deceit was growing deep, but she hadn't lied completely. She had taught the girls a thing or two.

A loud knock on the door interrupted the conversation and Desmond followed Evie downstairs.

She was thankful someone had disturbed Desmond's questioning.

When she opened the door, chaos ensued. Trevor was clearly upset, and Swifty was absolutely livid. The five children stood behind the two men with big eyes and closed mouths.

"How dare you tell those little girls to gang up on my sons!" Swifty screamed.

"My girls have bruises all over them!" Trevor shouted.

"My boys may not ever be right again! They sure ain't propagating or whatever you called it now!"

"Can you tell me why my girls pointed out where my *testicles* were when I picked them up?" Trevor demanded. "I was going to ignore the fact that I heard you betrothed by daughters to a bunch of future bikers, but this!"

Evie had no idea what to say or where to start, but Desmond had no problem expressing his emotions. He began laughing so hard he fell to the floor.

Down the street a loud commotion followed by two loud honks drew Desmond's, as well as the angry parents attention from Evie. Desmond began running toward the excitement, and Evie followed with Swifty, Trevor and all their children fumbling behind.

Jug smiled and waved as he drove down the street in none other than a yellow school bus marked 'Marshall County Schools.' The residents came running to see the excitement, and excitement it was. Jug was dog drunk and hooting out the window.

When he stopped and exited the bus, Desmond along with several other bikers loudly laughed, whooping and hollering along with their fellow club member. Evie furrowed her brow and shook her head at the incredibly large, inebriated man.

"You don't like my new wheels, Doc Stone?" Jug asked Evie.

"Why did you steal a bus?" she questioned.

"First off, I didn't steal this here bus. The way I see it, I own this bus being how there ain't many of us left and every week on my paycheck I used to see where I paid in for school taxes. I figure all of us own a bus, so I just went on over to the garage and picked up mine!" Jug cackled.

"What are you going to do with it?" Evie asked.

"Just wait and see, little lady!"

Evie found herself smiling at the large drunk man who had just been wheeling through town in a school bus. The distraction was just enough to give Evie a chance to run back to the big old house and away from any angry parents and Desmond's patronizing attitude, so she took the opportunity to quietly sneak away.

***

The week had passed slowly. Evie was exhausted from watching the children and setting up an exam room in one of the downstairs spare bedrooms of the new house she now called home. Other than her immediate family, children, ad anyone hurt or sick, Evie barely spoke to anyone. She felt as though she had somehow become persona non grata among a town that was run by a criminal motorcycle club. Although she made every effort to be kind, work hard and do her best to make amends to Trevor and Swifty, both men barely regarded her when they dropped off their children, and they even did that reluctantly.

It was Friday night, and Evie lay on her couch with her hands over her face. Not so long ago she would've looked forward to this time of the week. She'd have made plans with Sheena, unless she had to work the next day. Evie sighed. She missed working. She missed treating patients in the large hospital and wearing that white coat. Earning it had made her feel like a rockstar. Now she felt incompetent and worthless.

The supply run earlier in the week had been quite fruitful and Desmond along with Hazel, the diner owner, had decided the town was due for some much needed fun. Hazel, Retta and Birdie would prepare a special meal. Everyone in town with the exception of those who volunteered for guard duty had been invited to the first annual Survivor's Festival. According to Retta, it would be a jovial event with food and dancing. A few of the women, including Dani, had volunteered to decorate the street and everyone seemed excited. Everyone, except Evie.

She managed to drag herself off the sofa and into her bedroom. Evie opened the closet door to find a closet full of clothes, mostly too large or matronly for her to ever wear. There was nothing that was flattering or even remotely trendy at her disposal. Evie wanted to give up. She'd wanted so badly to find some normalcy in this horrible new world, be around people and have something to look forward to and when something finally happened, she was an outcast. The bikers were all quite upset with her, either because of Desmond or Swifty and she assumed everyone else gave her the cold shoulder because of Trevor and the mess she'd made of trying to teach his girls to stand up for themselves. Just when she decided that she wouldn't attend, someone knocked on her back door.

Evie peered out the glass to find no one on her back porch, but instead a huge box full of medical supplies like rubbing alcohol, hydrogen peroxide and half empty pill bottles. Evie rolled her eyes. At least she had something to keep her mind off the party. She'd organize the loot from the day's supply run while everyone else had a good time.

She dragged the large box inside to the pantry in the kitchen where she kept medications and began going through each one. Most of the bottles were almost empty, some of them expired and some of them probably useless. Many of the prescriptions were for depression and anxiety. She laughed. Everyone in town needed those.

As Evie made her way through the stuff, she also found some school supplies, colored pencils, crayons and notebooks. She'd use that stuff with the kids, but at the rate the children went through those things, they probably wouldn't last long. The girls loved to draw and color. Finally, when she got to the bottom of the cardboard container, Evie found a large, wrinkled brown paper bag. She opened it to find a cornflower blue dress with a single rose smashed on top.

Confused, Evie shook the dress out and held it to her body. It appeared as though it might fit nicely, but why had it been included in her supplies?

She smiled as she realized that her Uncle Del had been out on the supply runs earlier in the week and had probably found it and thought of her. It was unlike the man to make a gesture of that kind, but he had understood how disheartened she had been of late. Evie ran to the bedroom closet once again and began rummaging through the shoes. Although they were all about a half size too small, she did find one pair of white flip-flops that might not look quite as silly as her tennis shoes would with the outfit. Suddenly a renewed motivation came over Evie. She would attend the celebration, and somehow she would convince Trevor and everyone else not to be upset with her. She would have a good time.

Evie quickly began getting ready. The woman who had owned the house previously had some makeup that Evie could use, so she began digging through her bathroom vanity in search of anything that might spruce up her natural looks.

After applying a mauve lipstick, which was the only one that wasn't brown or orangey, she brushed through her hair and tied it up in a sloppy bun on the back of her head. Feeling a little adventurous, Evie stuck the rose in her hair and pinched her cheeks. The face that stared back from Evie in the mirror was one that was much prettier than she had looked in months, yet hardly what she expected once she made all the effort. She was skinny and she looked tired. Everyone did. Not letting the disappointment carry any further, Evie threw on the dress, rubbed at the wrinkles and skipped down the hallway as she headed toward Hazel's diner.

The street was filled with life. Brightly colored streamers of all colors hung from store windows and light posts. A few balloons were tied up here and there and one of the vehicles used for supply runs was parked in the street with music playing from the open windows.

The few children who Evie now knew by name were all playing around a sun-faded plastic swimming pool that was filled with plastic water guns and floating balls. They took turns throwing the balls to each other and splashing them in the pool.

The adults were smiling and talking as they mingled and snacked. The door to Hazel's diner was constantly jingling as residents entered and left. Evie was starving and quite curious as to what the special meal would be so she made her way there first.

Hazel, Retta and Birdie were chatting non-stop with everyone who walked in the door and pointing to all the delicious eats they had scrounged up for the festivity. Bowls full of trail mix, potato chips and some cookies were set out on one table, on another was a tray full of some sort of meat, Evie assumed to be probably squirrel and next to it, macaroni and cheese.

"Mac and cheese!" Evie shouted.

Retta, Birdie and Hazel stopped talking and began laughing.

"I told you Evie would just die when she saw that!" Retta informed Hazel.

Evie made a fast meal of a bowl of mac and cheese as Retta and Hazel discussed the good fortune of an earlier supply run bringing in several containers of powdered milk. Knowing she was most likely embarrassing her mother by her prison-style etiquette of eating, Evie slowly ate the last few bites she had scooped into her bowl and thanked the ladies for such a treat.

The smiles of her mother and grandmother warmed Evie's heart and she excitedly excused herself as she exited the diner to join the rest of the crowd on the street. Trevor stood on the sidewalk beside the diner, looking as dashing as she had seen him of late in a clean shirt and jeans with only a small tear in the knee. As she looked around she noticed everyone had done their best to dress for the occasion.

"Wow, Evie you look very nice," Trevor complimented.

"Thanks, you too!" She smiled and breathed in sigh of relief that her old friend no longer seemed to be upset with her.

"The girls are really having fun," Trevor pointed to his little angels as they splashed and played around the kiddie pool.

"This was a great idea."

"I think we all needed it. This is the most normal things have been since it all happened," Trevor smiled, but the gesture didn't quite reach his eyes. Evie wondered if he was thinking of his surely dead wife and the mother to his children.

Feeling a bit awkward, Evie looked away and noticed down the street, Desmond was walking her way with a huge smile on his face. He looked incredibly handsome with his blond, shaggy hair combed back and a cleanly shaven face she hadn't seen on him since her arrival.

Evie excused herself and began walking toward Desmond, running through what she might say to him in her mind. He was the one who had come up with this wonderful event and she wanted to thank him for all his efforts. She looked to him and offered a warm smile, which he returned a little to Evie's surprise.

As she neared him, her stomach fluttered a bit and she began to feel nervous. *"You clean up well,"* she could say. Or maybe she'd just tell him what a great idea he'd had. Not wanting to sound stupid, she decided on the latter. Just as the two were close enough Evie could speak to him without shouting, Dani blew by her and threw her arms around Desmond.

"Whoa Des, you look hot!" Dani purred.

Evie huffed and turned on her heel, immediately heading the other direction. She wasn't sure why she felt so irked, but she had an idea. Her uncle and Dani were right. She had developed some feelings for the man. *She was an idiot.*

"Evie, hold up!" Des yelled behind her, pushing Dani aside and chasing to catch up.

Evie kept walking, hastening her speed in an effort to get away.

"Hey!" Des shouted as he grabbed her by the arm. "I wanted to talk to you before everything got started here. Stop and talk to me."

"You're an ass. I've got nothing to say to you," Evie jerked away.

"I'm trying to make amends. Give me two seconds, please."

"I've given you too much already. Too much of my time, too much credit, too much everything. Go away."

Desmond nodded his head in a gesture that wasn't quite angry, but certainly not happy and Evie walked back to Trevor in hopes of continuing a more pleasant conversation.

Upon her return to Trevor the conversation was even more unpleasant than the one she'd just had with Des.

"When are you two going to stop this dumb crap and just get together?" Trevor laughed.

"What?" Evie questioned innocently.

"You and Des. A person would be blind not to see it. You like him," Trevor declared.

"Do not!"

"Don't deny it to me. I've known you forever. Stop acting like such a dork and tell him."

Evie hatefully glared at Trevor.

"You know he likes you too," Trevor grinned.

The blinding stinkface Evie focused on the man began to subside before she quietly asked, "What makes you think that?"

"I have eyes."

Evie shook her head at Trevor and punched him in the arm laughing.

"Now turn around and get a gander at the look he is giving me," Trevor told her.

Evie, as inconspicuously as possible, turned to find Desmond across the street staring a hole in through her friend.

"Do me a favor and find someone else to make him jealous now. I'm bigger than him, but he still scares me," Trevor confided.

Evie smiled and walked away with an extra pep in her step. Uncle Del and Jug were down the street standing by the confiscated school bus and Evie's curiosity overcame her. The hood of the bus was up and tools along with some large pieces of scrap metal were lying about on the ground next to the large vehicle.

As she approached, the two older men were discussing taking out windows and reinforcing the front of the bus with a ram guard.

"What are you going to do with this thing?" Evie asked.

"This here piss wagon is going to be the vehicle of choice for supply runs when I'm done!" Jug exclaimed, slapping his hand on the fender.

"What are you planning on doing with the seats inside of it?" Evie asked.

"We're going to take them out to make more room."

"Well, I think I could make use of them in the backyard of the house. The kids like to play and hang out back there, and we don't really have any lawn furniture."

"Nice idea, Hot Rod. We'll see what we can do!" Del answered.

Evie couldn't remember the last time she had seen her uncle so excited about anything.

"Is there anything I can do to help?" Evie offered.

Both men snickered a bit and shook their heads. Normally Evie would've been somewhat offended, but they were correct in their assumptions that she had no idea how to weld, work on a bus or generally fix anything like that.

Evie began to walk away, but turned instead, remembering her new dress, which had given her the confidence to join in the festivities.

"Thanks for the new duds, Uncle Del," Evie lilted as she twirled around, showing off her outfit.

"Girl, I don't know what you're talking about," Del quipped.

"This dress. Didn't you leave it for me?" Evie probed.

"Wasn't me," Del smiled knowingly and turned to Jug.

"You know, Des was wanting to talk to you. I think he had something important to tell you," Jug smirked.

Evie gave Jug a questioning look, but instead of explaining further he looked to her Uncle Delmont and the two men smiled even larger.

"I think the younger folks were heading on over to Des' place. You might try there," Jug suggested.

Evie made a silly face as she rolled her eyes as though she wasn't interested, but inside she was thoroughly intrigued. She looked around the area for anyone else to talk to so she wouldn't be tempted to go to Desmond's house, but the remaining residents of town that milled about were either younger kids or older adults. Her uncle was clearly busy with Jug planning renovations to the school bus, and her mother and grandmother were keeping themselves very occupied with Hazel at the diner. Evie turned in an almost complete circle looking around for someone, anyone really with whom she could mingle, but options were very limited. Even Trevor had left.

Her feet seemed to make the decision for her, and although Evie fought the urge in her mind, she found herself walking at a somewhat fast pace to

Desmond's little blue house. A quick turn behind the old Health Department gave Evie a clear view of his residence. It was filled.

Guardrail and Dani were drinking on the front porch, a few of the other bikers hung around to the side of the house and music blared from the inside. Evie confidently ascended the steps up the porch and wasn't surprised to find Dani glaring at her with what she was sure was a warning. Evie smiled in return, but careful to make sure the girl understood it wasn't a welcoming one. To add insult to injury Evie then smiled at Guardrail and winked.

Before Evie could see Dani's reaction, she entered the house and was surprised to find Trevor and Desmond talking on the couch. Both men smiled at her as she approached, and Trevor was quick to excuse himself.

"Can we talk now?" Desmond asked.

"Sure," Evie answered.

Des led her to the backyard where a small fire burned in a makeshift fire pit. Dusk was quickly turning into night and the embers of the fire popped and glowed in a way that Evie could only describe as perfectly romantic. Of course, she realized that at this moment anything might seem a bit romantic. After Trevor's insights and her Uncle's denial of the gift dress, Evie assumed this was the night that Desmond might actually express his feelings and put an end to his hot and cold behavior.

"It was really important for me to talk to you tonight. I'd first like to apologize for the way I have been treating you," Des began.

Evie smiled and let him continue.

"When you walked into the house and saw what you saw, I just felt like I needed to explain. There is nothing going on with Dani. When everything first happened, she had some addiction problems. Most of our club members and hang-arounds like that didn't make it long. It's hard to stay alive when you're out of your mind addicted to meth," Des explained. "Anyway, Guardrail and I helped her through some things, but that night she was having a rough time and had been drinking. I didn't kiss her back, and I'm quite certain she didn't mean to kiss me. Guardrail, of course, doesn't know any of this and if he did, I can only imagine how upset he would be at me and her. You get what I'm saying?"

Evie shook her head in agreement. She did understand and she had no intention of ever repeating what she had seen, but she disagreed with his assumptions. She was unequivocally certain that kiss had meant something to Dani.

"So again, I apologize for that and moving forward I hope that you won't hold my behavior toward you or that incident against me because I really think the two of us could make a really good thing here," Desmond added.

"So you've been thinking about us?" Evie asked, beaming from Desmond's disclosure. "Me too."

"Together with the club, your uncle, Trevor and Hazel, I think we could really make this a really good thing."

Confused, Evie considered his words in her head before she spoke.

"Excuse me? What do the others have to do with anything?" Evie asked confounded.

"The committees. Your uncle explained, right? That each of us would oversee committees for what we do, you being the local doctor, you know, you would be in charge of the health and wellness of the residents."

"Oh, of course, happy to help," Evie mumbled, her demeanor changing completely as she tried to recover from an embarrassing moment. She felt utterly stupid as she had assumed he'd meant to propose a different type of relationship.

"What's wrong?" Desmond questioned.

"Nothing, it's a wonderful idea," Evie attempted a smile, but she could tell it wasn't fooling Desmond.

Desmond furrowed his brow in seeming contemplation of her reaction.

"Wait. If your uncle didn't talk to you yet, what did you think I was talking about?"

"Something like that. Great idea. I'm really proud of you for wanting to make this a better place," Evie paused. "I should go."

"What's the rush?" Desmond asked.

"There was still some macaroni left at Hazel's," Evie blurted.

Desmond began laughing, and Evie cringed. Sometimes she really didn't think before she spoke and that was the first thing that came to mind. She did, in fact, plan on going straight to Hazel's but actually saying that sounded so ridiculous.

"I love cheese. Especially macaroni and cheese," Evie added to her horror. *Why couldn't she stop talking!* She was horrible in these situations. This was exactly why she hadn't had many boyfriends.

"I actually wanted to talk to you about more, but far be it for me to keep you away from powdered, cheesy pasta," Des chortled.

Gunshots rang out in the distance toward the northern barricade interrupting Evie's embarrassment and Desmond's amusement. They both began running through the backyard and toward the street.

For the last week, the north side of town had been relatively quiet. Evie now lived closer to that side of town, and she had begun to rest easier and get several hours of sleep each night. Although Desmond ran straight toward the action, Evie veered down an alley toward her house. Lying against her backdoor, Evie had left her baseball bat.

She grabbed the aluminum bat and raced toward the barricade which was only about a block from her home. The guards on duty had shot several rounds, but as Evie neared the fast pops of a semi-automatic grabbed her attention. *How many rotters could there be?* She wondered.

Desmond stood atop the barricade with Swifty and Scoop. Each of the men were taking calculated and accurate shots, to conserve ammo, Evie was sure, but more and more of the rotters seemed to turn the corner each second. Around twenty were now in the street coming down the hill toward the barricade, but Evie feared if they kept shooting, they'd not only waste ammo but draw the attention of even more.

"Too much noise!" Evie shouted as she scaled the wall of the bulwark to join Desmond. "Stop shooting!"

Evie grabbed the edge of the fence and began clambering down the side of the barricade into the street. She could hear shouts behind her, but didn't stop or even turn to look behind her.

She sprinted up the street until she neared the first zombie. Planting her feet, Evie took a big swing and crushed the thing's head like an overripe watermelon. It seemed somehow easier than the last time she had beat one.

The rotters were looking much worse than they had. Flesh hung off some of their faces, most of their skin was no longer pale like that of a corpse but more brown and gray. They stunk. The smell made Evie laugh. It was reminiscent of long car trips with her Uncle Del who ate copious amounts of beef jerky and unapologetically passed gas, a sort of mixture between death and feces. It was horrible, yet somehow hilarious.

From one zombie to the next, Evie smashed their heads, wielding her bat like a Samurai would his sword. That was how she imagined it, all very cool and sexy-like. The reality was most likely entirely different, but Evie didn't care. She was in a killing zone. The older zombie heads popped on contact with a decent swing. The ones that looked a little fresher took quite a bit more effort. She was quickly learning how hard to hit them and working her way through the sparse horde, when a shot rang out and a squishing thud landed at her heels.

Evie spun to see her Uncle Delmont with rifle in hand give her a nod from atop the bulwark and Desmond tearing toward her as she noticed a dead rotter at her feet she hadn't seen come up behind her.

"What the hell is wrong with you? You're going to get yourself killed!" Desmond shouted.

"You were going to get us all killed. You were being too loud with all the shooting. Noise attracts them," Evie explained and quickly began clubbing the remaining zombies.

"We are going to talk about this," Des growled as he jerked the bat from her hands and finished the last few off for her.

Walking back to the barricade, Evie realized almost the whole town was standing around the fences watching. As she neared she could hear them whispering.

"Was she laughing as she was killing those things?" someone asked.

"She did a better job than the bikers do, even if she is crazy."

Evie looked to Des and it was clear he had heard the comment as well. His reaction was similar to hers. He was obviously displeased.

Evie pushed past the crowd, but was grabbed by a strong small hand. It was Retta. Without saying a word, the woman grabbed her much taller daughter and pulled her tight without a word. It was clear to Evie the look in her mother's eyes was relief that she was still alive, but mostly shock and anger. Hopefully Del would help straighten things out later.

Evie pulled away, but kissed her mother on the cheek.

"Mama, I'm tired," Evie sighed. Her pace quickened and she began running home.

***

Evie flopped on her couch, smashing a pillow against her face, she screamed. For months she had held it together, if not for herself for her family. She was quickly unraveling. For twenty-seven years motivation and ambition had gotten her to the top of her class, an admission to medical school and eventually a white jacket and stethoscope. Now was the time all that hard work was supposed to be paying off and the rest of her life would be easier. She should be thinking about opening her own practice, making the big bucks and buying a huge house. Instead, right as the light at the end of the tunnel was near, the world decided to take a crap on her and all her hard work was for naught.

Evie shook her head, trying to convince herself that she was in fact one of the lucky ones, a survivor, yet the pity party had set up and was going full force. She looked down in disgust realizing that her new dress now had noxious-smelling, brown stains splattered all over it from the putrid corpses she had beaten.

She screamed again, this time without the pillow to muffle the sound.

A knock on the door interrupted her tantrum only to fuel her rage even more. Dealing with a concerned family member, an angry biker or someone dropping off a child was the last thing she felt like doing. Even though, Evie stomped her way to the door swinging it open in indignation to whomever might be waiting outside.

To Evie's great surprise, it was Dani. Evie's bat lay next to the doorjamb and she quickly leaned against the screen hiding the fact she was reaching for the weapon.

"What do you want?" Evie acerbically asked.

"Can I come in?" Dani calmly answered.

"Why?"

"To talk," Dani responded.

"About what?"

"Just let me in!" Dani's placid demeanor faltered.

Hesitantly, Evie opened the door and sarcastically held out her hand in a motion for the girl to enter, resting the bat behind a nearby chair.

Dani looked around the residence, strolling through the house as though she owned it, eventually making her way to Evie's living room and promptly plopping down on the couch.

"You got anything to drink?" Dani asked.

"Like what?"

"I thought maybe Jug might've brought you over some of his shine. He says its medicine."

"Why do you want that? Are you sick or do you want to get loaded and try to force yourself on Des again? It didn't look like it worked to well last time," Evie contended.

"Stay away from Desmond," Dani barked.

"Or what?" Evie blurted out with no control over her own mouth.

"I won't just fight you, I'll come in here while you're asleep and I'll kill you."

"From what I've seen of your hummingbird ass, it hardly backs up that mocking bird mouth of yours," Evie smirked as her uncle's vernacular unintentionally spilled from her mouth. Slowly Evie reached behind the chair for the handle of her baseball bat.

Dani jumped from the sofa, pulling a knife from the waistband of her pants.

Evie tightly gripped the bat and choked up on the handle.

"I would get that idea out of that stupid head of yours, Dani Creepshow. Now get out of my house 'cause I'm fixin' to brain you."

Dani stormed through the living room and out the door and Evie began to laugh. *'Cause I'm fixin' to brain you?* She had certainly lost quite a bit of accent living in Ohio for as long as she had, but nothing like what she'd just said had ever escaped her lips even before she moved. Apparently hanging out with a bunch of crazy bikers and the likes of Dani had pushed her to a new level or lowered her level of vocabulary exponentially.

Evie's amusement lasted for only a short time before she realized Dani had threatened to kill her in her sleep and she had done nothing but made that situation worse by egging her on. The rest of the night Evie gripped her bat and dared not shut her eyes.

CHAPTER FOURTEEN

Evie dressed and began her day just as she normally did, only much slower. She lumbered through the house trying to remember each thing she needed to do before she went to grab a quick breakfast at Hazel's. There was something different about a normal sleepless night and a sleepless night where one was terrified they would be slaughtered in their sleep, Evie decided. Each creak in the old house had put her on edge. Eventually she would learn to keep her mouth shut and head down, she hoped.

The worn cotton dress Evie threw on felt like fiberglass insulation rubbing against her skin and her hair felt dirtier and greasier than normal. The back of her neck was still wet with sweat from the scratchy pillow she had attempted to sleep on all night. This would be the perfect time for an espresso, Evie concluded. The zombie apocalypse really sucked for so many reasons.

After a half-hearted attempt at brushing her teeth, Evie made her way out the door and down the street to the diner. It seemed unseasonably hot, especially after she entered the small restaurant with most of the town in attendance.

To her surprise, Priest was also there, looking pale and sweaty. She had made sure that he had plenty of supplies to manage his diabetes, but suspected that he was rationing what the supply run guys had brought him. Although she knew it was making him sick, she couldn't blame him for trying to make it last, but it wouldn't work that way. She would need to speak with him.

Next to him at the table up front sat Desmond, Jug and her Uncle Delmont, who smiled and motioned for her to join him when she entered. Evie looked around the diner, expecting more whispers and awkward stares but what she found instead was a quiet and strange awe from the other survivors. Many smiled and patted her on the back as she walked by to join the men.

"What's going on?" Evie whispered as she took a seat next to her uncle.

"We are voting for a city council," Del whispered back.

Priest rose and the few that were softly talking or eating abruptly stopped.

"With so many of us, and our numbers growing, the town needs to be more organized. I have agreed to share the responsibility of leading with some others, people who we are gonna vote for today. There are many things that need to be done 'round here to make sure we survive, and we are going to make committees and elect someone to oversee each one."

Some of the townspeople began whispering back and forth, and Evie heard her name mentioned more than once. She hoped the people weren't questioning her ability to be a competent doctor after her theatrics the night before. Desmond had already made it clear that she would be the person in charge of medicine and caring for the sick.

"First let's start off with one of our most important roles. Someone needs to be in charge of rationing food and making sure our people eat. I nominate Hazel with Retta Stone and Birdie Tucker on that committee," Priest continued.

Hazel who was flitting about like a chicken with her head cut off emptying pans and picking up dishes stopped in her tracks and stared at the grizzled biker in disbelief. Priest's amusement was palpable when he noticed her reaction, but quickly recovered his somber demeanor.

"I second the nomination!" A voice in the back yelled.

Quickly another person chimed in their agreement, then another and another.

"Those who agree Hazel should be our Council Lady in charge of food, raise your hand," Priest instructed.

The entire restaurant lifted their hands.

"I don't see a point in asking if anyone objects, so there you have it. Hazel is our first council member."

Applause and well-wishes erupted and Hazel smiled, looking a bit terrified.

"Moving on," Priest interrupted the crowd. "The next seat will be for our supply run leader. This nomination needs to be for someone we trust not to steal for themselves, someone who can handle themselves outside of our walls and they will be in charge of getting and distributing supplies for the town. Would anyone like to make a nomination?"

Almost instantaneously Dani rose and shouted, "I nominate myself!"

Snickers erupted and someone from the back of the room shouted, "The only thing she is good at getting and distributing is crabs and crack!"

Priest rolled his eyes and reluctantly asked, "Does anyone second the nomination?"

A long moment passed before a little old lady in the back who Evie had only seen in passing rose and declared, "I think it should be Evie Stone. She is fair and can handle herself better than any of you men with those monsters!"

"I second the nomination!"

"Third!"

"Evie Stone!" The room began shouting.

"Wait! Shut yer mouths for a minute!" Priest screamed.

When the room became quiet Priest continued, "Evie is our town doctor. No one else is capable of doing that job. You can't be a council member for more than one committee. Does anyone object to Evie being the person in charge of our sick and the medicine?"

"She's good at killing too!" Swifty hollered.

"Yes, she is. So are lots of us. No one else is good at killing and curing though, now are they?" Priest challenged.

Without hesitating or asking for the residents to vote, Priest immediately declared Evie the councilperson handling all things medically related.

Within a half an hour, all the council seats had been filled, each of them by Soldiers of Chaos members with the exception of Evie, Hazel, Trevor, who would oversee all construction projects and her uncle Delmont who ended up being in charge of hunting and providing fresh meat. With no surprise to Evie, Priest himself also sat on the council with no real committee to head yet still in a leadership position.

If anyone truly believed that the townspeople would get a fair vote on anything, they were sorely mistaken. The gang members would obviously back each other's vote and outnumber anything they didn't want. No one seemed to be terribly disgruntled about the election, with the exception of Dani, however, and even Evie was somewhat pleased by the morning's events since two elderly women who shared a residence several houses down from Evie had been chosen to oversee the daycare so that Evie might focus more on all things medical.

Evie's excitement toward her new role seemed to work better than any espresso. She almost skipped out the door of the diner until she was spun in the opposite direction by a firm hand on her shoulder. Evie was face to face with Desmond, who reciprocated her huge smile.

"So I guess you are happy now?" He asked.

"Yes, those eggs were fantastic," Evie quipped.

"The eggs, right. The same tired powdered eggs we've had all week. I guess that's it, not the fact that you won't have to deal with those little heathen rugrats anymore, right?"

"If I say that, does that sound just awful?" Evie whispered, still smiling.

"What would you care if it did?" Desmond joked.

"You're right, I wouldn't. I am thrilled I can focus on the one thing I wanted to do with my life and not listen to those little snots scream all day!"

Desmond laughed, a real laugh even, not one of those sarcastic chuckles Evie had come to know and hate, but a laugh so genuine that it lit up even his eyes.

The tiny amount of tension that still inhabited Evie's shoulders and neck seemed to melt away and in that moment nothing else seemed to matter. Not the fact that she hadn't had tooth floss in weeks, that her hair felt like it had been soaked in bacon grease, not even the fact that there were splatters of brains still left on her shoes, Evie felt joy, and began laughing with him.

"You look so happy," Desmond said.

"I think this is the first time I've felt truly normal or happy since this all started. For once I don't feel out of control, hopeless and weak."

Desmond threw his arm around her and kissed her on the forehead.

"Strength does not come from physical capacity. It comes form an indomitable will."

"Is that Ghandi?" Evie asked incredulously.

"What? Don't look at me like that. I read crap too," Des declared.

"*You read crap too?* Whew. I thought we had pod people and not just zombies there for a minute!" Evie laughed.

Desmond put her in a light choke hold with his arm and rubbed her hair with his fist, "You think you're so funny, don't you?"

"Hilarious, in fact I..." Evie trailed her sentence off when she spied Dani staring from down the street with a look of hate so exaggerated it actually sent cold chills down her spine.

"What's wrong?" Des asked and began scanning the area.

"Nothing. I should get moving. I want to set up another exam room and reorganize my pantry with medical supplies. Now that the house isn't a daycare I can make it into a more suitable clinic," Evie coldly informed him, purposefully seeming frigid and unresponsive to their previous flirtations as she backed away.

"Okay, sure," Des threw his hand back in a surrendering type motion, his affront obvious.

Evie wasted no time getting back to her house, half expecting to find Dani waiting for her there. When she was sure she was alone, she crept outside to the back porch with her baseball bat and a tiny cupful of Jug's moonshine. Jug, had in fact, dropped off a gallon of it, claiming it had medicinal properties from healing arthritis to curing the common cold.

Evie knew the concoction would have no real healing properties, but she did hope it would make her chest feel like I gorilla wasn't sitting on it.

Evie shrank to the top step of the porch and sat cross-legged staring, then sniffing the potent homebrew.

"That'll put some hair on your chest."

Evie jerked her head up, splashing the moonshine all over her clothes, to find Desmond with a perplexed look on his face.

"I'm not going to drink it!"

"Then what exactly were you doing with it?" He asked.

"Okay, I was going to drink it."

"What's up with you? You're drinking moonshine after breakfast and I don't even know what just happened in the street."

"You want to know what happened now? After all you've done to ignore it and even make it worse?" Evie asked.

"Woman, again, what is up?" Des asked.

"Dani Creepshow is what's up. I'm tired of her constant crap and having to sleep with one eye open!"

Desmond laughed.

"You think this is funny?" Evie's voice began to rise.

"I think it's been such a long time since I've been around a woman I forgot how overdramatic you people can be."

"When one of us is dead, will that be dramatic enough for you?"

"Evie, come on now. Dani is just a pain in the ass, but nothing more. Neither of you is going to kill the other," Desmond reasoned.

"Funny, that's not what she promised me last night when she came into my house and told me if I didn't stay away from you that she'd kill me in my sleep," Evie ranted then sloshed the bit of moonshine down her throat.

"She did? And that's why I've been getting this hot and cold treatment from you lately? Because she threatened you?" Desmond growled.

"Every time you are near me she is skulking about giving me stinkeye. I'm tired enough of fighting to stay alive from everything else in this world that is trying to kill me, I don't need a sociopathic skank added to my problems. Just because she has some misguided perception you are in love with me."

"It's not misguided," Des confessed.

He rose, grabbed Evie by the hand and jerked her upright so violently that she dropped the small cup that had contained the ill-tasting moonshine. Before Evie could protest he was dragging her across the yard and into the street. She could barely keep up without her feet falling behind and losing her footing.

"Des, where the heck are we going?" Evie demanded.

"I'm settling this now."

Desmond, with Evie stumbling behind him, stalked past Hazel's, her family's residence in the old giftshop and finally made their way to the Southern barricade where they found Guardrail and Jug, sitting atop the wall laughing and cleaning their weapons.

"Brother, need you down here now," Desmond demanded of his fellow biker.

Desmond's displeasure could be read all over his face, and both Guardrail and Jug, seemed reluctant to ask which brother he was referring.

"Guard, down here now," Desmond clarified with little patience.

"Bro, what's going on?" Guardrail asked as he descended the barricade.

"Your woman, she has family alive in Possum Trot, true?" Desmond asked.

"Yeah, last we heard her sister was still hanging in there with her family."

"You need to take her there and drop her off. I want her out today. Feel me?" Desmond commanded.

"Whoa, I can't take her out there and just leave her, man!" Guardrail argued.

"Last night she busted up in Evie's place and threatened to kill her," Desmond informed his buddy.

"She ain't gonna kill nobody, dude. You know she's all talk," Guardrail attempted to reason.

"Would it make a difference if I told you your woman has been trying to crawl up on me for months?"

Guardrail's face fell and a look of disbelief washed over him. He squinted his eyes as if in thought, finally settling on Desmond's face and asked, "You being real with me?"

"I'm sorry, man. She's no good for anyone, you need to take her away from here."

"Screw that, I'll drop her off outside of town and let the dead have her. Why should I do that slut any favors?" Guardrail decidedly spoke.

"You can't just take her out and leave her to die!" Evie urged.

Desmond slid his hand down Evie's arm until his palm lay flat against hers and he clasped her hand. Evie turned her attention from Guardrail to Desmond just in time to notice him give her a quick wink and a slight shrug.

"Dude, how about this? You take the skank back home to her family, and I'll see what I can do about hooking you up with Kim. She's been giving you the eye."

"Kim, that soccer mom with the busted teeth on cleaning crew?"

"No, man! Kim that used to work at the Beaver Trap, you know the one that always danced to 'Cherry Pie?'"

"Right! The one Chicken calls butterface!" Guardrail once again squinted his eyes and stared at the ground for a long moment before raising his face, sporting a huge smile. "It is the end of the world. Beggars can't be choosers, right? I can always throw a bag on her head!"

The men burst with laughter until Desmond turned to look at Evie. She was certain the look on her face exhibited her utter indignation towards the men and the conversation that had just occurred. Not to mention she was a little more than disgusted that Desmond seemed to be all too familiar with the staff members of the local strip club.

"Okay, man. I'll get her gone," Guardrail agreed.

"Thanks, bro," Desmond slapped his comrade's back and began to turn and walk away, tugging on Evie's hand to follow.

"Yo, Des!" Jug hollered as they walked away. "There any more of those nudey dancers you can hook me up with?"

Des didn't turn around but waved his free hand as he shouted, "See what I can find, bro!"

Evie's mouth dropped and she suddenly stopped dead in her tracks.

"What?" Des chuckled.

"How is it that you know those, those... exotic dancers?" She interrogated.

"I know everybody, baby, doesn't mean I know them as well as your thinking," Desmond smirked.

Evie almost forgot why she was irritated as she melted into his crooked grin.

CHAPTER FIFTEEN

Earlier that afternoon Evie hung a note on her door that read, "Out of the Office." Desmond knew where to find her in case of an actual emergency, but she had hoped to have an afternoon off so that she might spend some quality time with her favorite uncle.

Retta and Birdie would be at the diner all day gossiping and preparing food with Hazel for another special dinner, but Del didn't have guard duty or any supply runs, so the two sat in the backyard of the old gift shop by the creek talking shop.

"We're about to run out of necessities. The supply runs are lookin' sadder every day, Hot Rod," Del confided.

"I didn't think things were that bad since Hazel is planning another big supper tonight. Once we deplete the rest of the resources from the remaining nearby houses, what will we do?" Evie asked.

"The dinner tonight is because some of the goods we've found are about to go bad and Hazel wanted to use them up. I'm not sure what we'll do when it's all gone, but the only way this many people can stay alive in one place is if we start farming and providin' for ourselves," Del answered.

"Attempting to farm would be dangerous unless we cleared a very large area of any rotters, and we haven't even started. We're not going to have food through the winter, are we?"

"What we've been stockpiling might get us through, but it will be close and people are going to be a might hungry. I want you to know, when I go out huntin', I go back to the cabin and mow the airstrip too."

Evie paused. She understood his meaning. Uncle Del was making a backup plan for their family. If things got bad, they would leave.

"Where would we go?" She asked.

"Not a clue. We'd have to find somewhere to land where we could stay or refuel. Not sure where either one of those things could happen. Anywhere we landed might be dangerous. But the good news is, I can fly again if we need. No restrictions can stop me now. Nobody to enforce them!" Del laughed.

It didn't seem like that much of a bright side, but Evie smiled and laughed with him. She knew how her uncle had missed being a pilot.

A moment later, Evie heard faint voices from the street in front of their new home. A deep cackle grabbed her attention and she strained to confirm it was in fact, the only person she had ever heard make such a horrendous sound.

Evie rose and quietly moved to the side of the house to get a view. Dani and Guardrail were traversing the barricade. As the two climbed over, Evie eavesdropped.

"It's about time you guys let me go out on supply runs!" Dani said happily.

"This is actually more of a drop off than any kind of pick up," Guardrail corrected.

"Huh?"

"Just get in the car, skank. I gotta be back here before dinner."

"I hear it's gonna be a fancy dinner again! We got something good for supper tonight?" Dani asked.

Guardrail laughed. "Oh yeah, your supper is going to be a big surprise."

Evie was amazed the girl didn't seem to be suspicious or upset at the circumstances. She truly was as dumb as Evie had assumed. Guardrail would be coming back to town alone, and poor Dani didn't have the first inclining it seemed.

Evie wanted to feel guilty about having the girl banished from the safety of the town, but she couldn't. She breathed easier and she could feel an involuntary smile creep across her face.

"Ain't no room for a trouble-makin' rounder like that in this new world of ours, at least not our town," Del voiced, startling Evie as he had crept up behind her unbeknownst.

"You knew?" Evie questioned.

"Not 'til just now. Dumb ole girl don't even realize he's dumpin' her off. He gonna put her in a sack and throw her over a bridge like a cat nobody wanted?" Del asked.

"No! Of course not!" Evie responded. "She has family that may still be alive, so he is taking her to them."

"We ain't seen nobody new in a long time. Lots can happen. Don't you go feelin' soft if you find out that ole girl is on her own and get any notions about savin' her. I seen the way she looks at you. She's a gunnin' for you, Ev. Let this be."

Evie nodded and returned to her seat in the backyard. She hadn't considered Dani's family might be gone or most likely dead. She let that idea settle for a moment waiting for the gravity of the thought to sink in. *Nope, still no guilt.*

"So about the pretty boy," Del teased.

"What about the pretty boy?" Evie asked with a bit of an angered tone.

"Don't you sass me, young lady!" Del laughed. "And don't you avoid the question."

"What question?"

"You ready to admit you're sweet on him yet?"

"What if I were?" Evie retorted.

"I'd tell you I still think he's a might pretty for a man with that shaggy girl hair, but he's growin' on me."

"You want me to date Priest's nephew, a Soldier of Chaos?" Evie asked incredulously.

"They ain't exactly lining up knockin' down the door anymore, and he sure is tryin' hard. He came by this morning with some sparkly baubles for your mom and granny. He got on their good side quick."

"He did what?" Evie gasped.

"Said he found the jewelry on a run and thought it'd be mighty pretty on 'em, so now they're over at Hazel's lookin' like the Queens of England!"

"So Mom and Granny think I should date him too now, huh?"

Del laughed.

"They decided the only other option is that Thomas boy and he may still be married if his wife ain't dead and that wouldn't be right. Plus he's got three children already. Personally, I agree. I kinda believe he might be the sissiest thing I ever seen. He's a big fella, but he sure is a scaredy cat."

Evie laughed again, but this time a real laugh. It was true. Trevor had always been a bit of a wuss.

Evie rose and hugged her uncle.

"I should check on the clinic, but I'll catch up with you at dinner," Evie promised, kissing her uncle on the cheek.

She began walking back to her house and clinic with a new outlook on life. The food cooking from Hazel's diner smelled a little tastier. The sky appeared a little more blue than usual. The music coming from Jug's garage was, well, it was just awful outlaw country music, but Evie didn't care and danced down the street to the beat. Life would be so much better without Dani Creepshow.

As Evie approached her house, she spied one of her fellow residents waiting for her on the porch. As she neared, she recognized the girl, but didn't know her name. She was a member of the cleaning committee, which meant at times, she had to remove corpses from the new parts of the encampment as it grew. Evie didn't envy her job.

"Hey Doc Stone!" the girl enthusiastically spoke.

"Hey, um," Evie struggled, however, was unsure she had ever heard the girl's name before, which made her question if she shouldn't get to know all the residents better and start files on each.

"Kim. It's Kim," the girl smiled.

"Of course, sorry, Kim," Evie apologized. "What can I do for you?"

"Can we go inside? It's personal and all," Kim whispered.

Evie ushered Kim into her house and motioned for her to head back to a large utility room that Evie now had set up as her exam area.

"So what's going on?" Evie asked.

"Well, I got this hot date tonight and I could use some advice. The disposable razor I've been using is two months old. I tried shavin' under my arms, you know, in anticipation of tonight, then I splashed some of this old perfume under there to maybe smell a little fresher and it burnt like fire!" Kim raised her arm to demonstrate and show Evie the results of her efforts.

Evie threw a hand up and with exaggeration winced, then giggled a bit.

"Oh girl, that is the worst razor burn I've seen. Ouch. I don't have anything here that could help with the bumps, and I can't spare any aspirin for pain, but you can head down to Hazel's and ask if they have any apple cider vinegar or honey that you could use. If they do, gently rub some on it. Oh, and throw away that razor."

"Thanks doc!"

"Not to be nosey, but the hot date tonight, wouldn't happen to be with Guardrail, would it?" Evie curiously asked.

"How'd you know?" Kim beamed.

"Small town, you know. Word travels fast," Evie answered.

"That and I expect you probably heard from Desmond. Everybody 'round here knows the two of you are getting a case up."

"They do?" Evie questioned, a bit shocked to actually hear it form someone other than her extremely observant uncle.

"Well, I imagine they do. I see how he looks at you. Plus he's the one who told me to come here and get checked out when he set me up with Guardrail while ago. He ain't foolin' nobody trying to hide he's sweet on you. You can hear it in his voice every time he says your name or talks about you."

"Are the two of you close friends?" Evie asked.

"I don't know that I'd call us friends, but he sure has done a lot for me."

Jealousy manifested in a hot flush of stomach acid that rose up Evie's chest and into her throat. Evie imagined Kim circling around a pole half-naked. Before Evie knew her, not so long ago. She had worked as a dancer. One of the many that Des seemed to be all too acquainted with from the Beaver Trap.

"Like what?" Evie finally asked.

"Well, my ex used to ride with the SOC and one night he drank too much and beat the hell out of me. I was in the hospital for four days, and I looked so bad I couldn't work for two weeks after that for all the bruises. Des helped me out so I didn't get behind on bills and made sure that it never happened again."

"How did he do that?" Evie asked, but immediately regretted, unsure if she wanted to know the answer.

"Des ran him out of town. He ain't been back since, he even left his bike at my house. Des told me I could sell it to pay for my hospital bills, so I did!" Kim smiled.

Evie returned her smile, but was sure there was a certain amount of unease that read across her face at the idea Kim's ex seeming to be missing and leaving expensive property. At the same time, she felt a huge amount of relief that Desmond was only a good Samaritan helping out an abused woman, stripper or not.

CHAPTER SIXTEEN

The feast was in full swing, and Evie could hardly contain her joy. Her face ached from smiling, and she laughed from deep inside each time her Uncle Del or Jug told a wild boot camp story or Retta made an ugly face at her brother for retelling his wild youth.

Tables were set around outside Hazel's, much like the festival the night before, but this time there was one very distinct difference. The music blared not from one of the supply run vehicles, but instead Jug's stolen school bus that he had that very day reinforced with loads of sheet metal and a makeshift plow on the front, and obviously one insane sound system blasting Jug's trademark outlaw country music. He had welded bits of chicken wire and in places, chain link fencing around most of the windows. It was an unbelievable feat of recycled mechanics, but something that Evie believed would be a great asset for hauling goods back from longer, more dangerous supply runs. As she looked the vehicle over, her smile grew even larger. Her uncle and Desmond would have a safer mode of transportation in the giant hunk of repurposed school bus.

Life was coming back together, and although the next few months would be difficult, Evie was certain the town would figure out how to make it through winter. The bus would certainly help, and as she gazed around everyone in town seemed to be happy and more than willing to not only work to take care of themselves but each other.

Groups of people who most likely would've never taken the time to know each other were sitting together and laughing. Trevor and his three girls sat with Swifty, Scoop and their children, who were all playing together. Hazel and Priest stood by the buffet line chatting and smiling, and just to the edge of the larger tables toward the Southern barricade, sat Kim and Guardrail on a blanket together.

As Evie glanced in her direction, Kim waved and motioned for her to come over. Evie reciprocated the wave and excused herself from the table making her way to the romantic picnic style seating her patient occupied.

"Doc Stone!" Kim excitedly hollered, grabbing Evie by the hand as she got close, and pulled her down to the pallet.

"How are you guys?" Evie asked.

"Great! I told Guardrail we should share our good fortune with you!" Kim exclaimed as she reached into a duffle and pulled out a tupperware bowl.

"What's that?"

Kim carefully opened the container and inside was a mix of hard candies, some in wrappers and some not, a few of them appearing melted and stuck together.

"I've been hoarding some of the goodies we find on supply runs that the other guys don't want or Hazel can't use. It's not much, but sometimes you just get a hankering for some sweets, ya know?" Guardrail smiled sweetly, unlike Evie had ever seen on his face. "Have one if you want it."

Hating to refuse a kind gesture, Evie managed to pick out a wrapped candy and put it in her mouth. She moaned a bit when the sugar began to melt. The new couple laughed.

"I had forgotten how much I miss candy. Thank you so much!" Evie sincerely showed her appreciation.

"It's not much, but if you had gotten to be a doctor in the old world, you'd have been making big bucks. I felt bad I didn't have anything to give you earlier so I wanted you to know how grateful I am for all you do for everybody," Kim replied.

Before Evie knew what she was even doing she hugged the girl. Although Kim had just paid her with a piece of candy and some kind words, it meant the world to Evie. Up until that morning, she had been so focused on what she had lost, she was starting to see how much more important her life could be now. Evie's eyes started to water and she blinked hard in an attempt to suppress any tears form actually falling down her face before she pulled back from her impromptu bear hug. Evie turned her head to wipe one that had escaped on her shoulder and loudly gasped at what she saw from just beyond the fence of the barricade.

Kim pushed Evie back with care, obviously realizing something was very wrong.

"Doc, why are you crying?" Kim asked with concern.

"Your gesture was just so sweet," Evie answered still staring past Kim toward the chain link fence.

"I know, right, Doc? I want to cry every time I eat a piece of candy too, it's so dang good!" Guardrail joked.

"Could we speak privately?" Evie asked the biker.

Kim looked a bit off-put by the request but said nothing and Guardrail nodded. Evie walked to the fence closest to where she had been focused earlier.

"I am sure I just saw Dani Krenshaw, out there," Evie declared.

"Nah, she's gone," Guardrail reassured.

"Gone as in you took her to her family's home, and they were alive and well and you dropped her off?" Evie grilled.

"Sure, if that's what you need to hear, Doc," Guardrail smiled, not the pleasant one he had just worn in the presence of Kim, but the one that held a bit of evil that Evie had seen often.

"What did you do with her?"

"Seriously, I was going to take her to Possum Trot, but when we got in the car, she started in again. Her family is a bunch of meth heads, and I know they aren't still alive, so I didn't see a point in risking my life to take her that far out. I got as far as the grocery in

Draffenville and told her we were going to check for supplies. I grabbed some candy that hadn't been looted and jumped in the car and left her there. There's no way she made it back here."

"You just left her?" Evie furiously asked.

"In a grocery store. There was some food. I thought it was pretty generous. I could've tied her to a tree out in the park," Guardrail smiled even bigger as though he was imagining the idea.

"Unbelievable," Evie sighed and stormed away in search of Desmond.

***

"He's right. There's no way that skank could've made it back from Draffenville this quick, or was stupid enough to leave the safety and supplies of a grocery," Des agreed.

"You are completely missing the point. He left her out there on her own. That's basically sentencing her to die, Des," Evie debated.

"Our people have to answer for their actions. There are consequences now. This isn't like life before,

Evie. Had you rather her still be in town and having to watch your back constantly?" Des reasoned.

"Of course not, but I'd have felt a lot better about the situation if she had been left with someone, or at least somewhere secure," Evie's voice calmed a bit as the idea of Dani's incessant threats rang in her head. She had been so much happier with the girl gone, as much as she hated to admit it to herself.

"Ev, I need to ask you something," Desmond suddenly seemed so serious.

"What?"

"How do you feel about me?"

Evie paused. She wasn't sure how to answer. Desmond had become so much more than just a fellow survivor or the guy in charge of their little town. He invaded her every thought. He was the first thing she usually thought of each morning and the last thing on her mind at night. He was nothing that she had ever wanted before, but everything to her now. How could she say those things to him?

"Could you see yourself with a guy like me? I know I'm not good enough for someone like you, but I'd do anything to keep you safe. Evie, I'm in love with you. I want to spend..."

Before he could finish his sentence, the moment Evie heard the word love, nothing else mattered. She kissed him.

Desmond grabbed her by the hand and began pulling her through yards and streets toward the celebration. When they reached Hazel's and the other townspeople, Desmond whistled.

"This is crazy," he began in a loud voice, "but I want everyone in town to hear this."

Everyone in the street became quiet, and Jug shut off the music blarring from the bus. Desmond still holding Evie's hand slowly lowered himself to one knee before her and began speaking again.

"Evie Stone, I know I don't deserve a woman like you, but if you will have me, I'll work every day to become the man you need. Marry me?"

Evie could no longer feel her face. Her knees began to buckle and the hand Des held shook so hard she was certain she'd shake him loose. She began to speak but nothing came out.

"Maybe I can sweeten the deal with this," Desmond added and with his free hand pulled a ring box from his pocket.

Still holding her hand, he pried the box lid open revealing an enormous square stone.

"Yes," Evie replied, so quickly and matter of fact-like, she even shocked herself.

Des slid the ring on her finger and rose to his feet giving her a short kiss and big hug.

"I refuse to let anyone call me your 'Old Lady' though," Evie demanded.

The town erupted in laughter, whistles and cheers. Jug, Swifty and Scoop ran to the couple, pulling Evie away from Desmond and lifted her into the air as they hollered and spun her around.

The festivities had become an impromptu engagement party and someone turned the music back on, even louder than before.

Friends and family gathered around the couple to congratulate them and others danced in the streets, whether to celebrate Evie's engagement or Hazel's stockpile of oily peanut butter, Evie wasn't sure, nor did she care. She was happier than she had ever been and quickly forgot all about Dani Creepshow.

CHAPTER SEVENTEEN

It was later that night after the festivities had finally waned and all the residents returned to their homes that the excitement began to wear off and Evie realized what she had earlier excitedly agreed to do. Did she really want to marry Desmond Young? He was ridiculously attractive, strong, a great guy to have around during the current state of world, but as a husband? She actually knew very little of what he had been doing the last few years. She knew very little about him at all. The unyielding loneliness of surviving had gotten to her, obviously. She couldn't up and marry him, could she?

Evie sat on her couch contemplating life with and without Des. She actually was pretty crazy about him, and what were the odds that she would ever meet anyone else that was close to her own age, attractive and intelligent? More than likely he was Benton's most eligible bachelor and would remain that way until she put a ring on it.

Evie gazed down at the enormous diamond on her hand. It had to be three carats. She never cared much for things like that or even thought much about her own wedding like most girls did, but she had to admit, that ring sure was a stunner. Maybe she could prolong the engagement until she got to know him better and made a more informed decision, she concluded. Giving the ring back now would make everyone in town despise her and she wasn't quite ready to give up on him anyway. Part of her did want to spend the rest of her life with Desmond, however long or short that life might be.

Instead of dwelling on her indecision, Evie pulled herself up from the couch and picked up the latest supply run box which sat next to her front door. This one was extra heavy. She hoped it held more useful goodies than the last several.

Inside she found much of the same; rubbing alcohol, anti-diarrhea pills, laxatives, vitamins and some gauze among some natural remedies she had asked for the men to keep an eye out for including witch hazel, several bottles of lotions and some moisturizing creams. To Evie's surprise, in the pill bottles she found some very useful medications. One of which was an almost full bottle of vancomycin, a very strong antibiotic.

Evie categorized and began documenting how many of each she had in her ledger. She neatly stacked the lotions and creams on a shelf, but added the prescription meds to a lockbox Swifty had found for her weeks ago. Over time, Evie was accumulating a small stash of some medications that might be very useful, as well as some painkillers that she worried someone might steal. Although many of the meds were expired, they would still work.

When everything was neatly organized, Evie's watch read four a.m. She had certainly had a long and eventful day, but she still wasn't in the least bit tired. Retta and Birdie would be getting up to go to Hazel's and prepare breakfast soon, so Evie headed out the door in hopes of catching her mother and grandmother before they began their shift. They had both congratulated her and seemed so pleased the night before, but she wondered if their feelings might be a bit more honest when the rest of the town wasn't watching.

The street outside Evie's house was quiet with the exception of Chicken and Charlie Nunn at the northern barricade on guard duty. Charlie, one of the oldest residents, had proven himself quite the sharp shooter and wasn't in the best shape to do many other things but sit. Guard duty was the perfect job for him, however, Evie understood the guards preferred to be paired with anyone but Charlie. He was extremely hard of hearing in both ears and being partnered with him made for a long night.

Evie could hear Chicken repeating himself and loudly asking Charlie questions. The two men occasionally laughed and although it was difficult to communicate with Charlie, Chicken seemed to be enjoying his post. She laughed with them. What an odd couple those two were. No more odd than her and Des, she thought. The end of the world certainly brought people together who might've never given each other a chance.

As Evie strolled down the street, enjoying the time to herself and the quiet serenity of the early morning, a distant thumping caught her attention. She continued walking past the old Health Department where Priest lived, then past Hazel's, which was dark and quiet, yet the thumping sound grew. As Evie neared the old gift store where her mother, grandmother and uncle stayed, she recognized the beating noise to be bass drum, accompanied by other instruments and screeching vocals. It was heavy metal music blaring in the distance, just past the Southern barricade. Evie ran to join Swifty and Scoop who were leaning over the bulwark and Evie joined them in an effort to see where the music originated.

Down the street, a beat up old four-door coupe slowly idled toward them with a herd of rotters trailing behind and to each side. As it slowly neared, Evie panicked. Although Scoop and Swifty didn't seem to understand what to make of the dangerous visitor, Evie knew exactly what was happening.

"Shoot her!" Evie shouted.

Scoop turned to question Evie, but Swifty took aim and began firing. Bullets hit the door panel and window of the rustbucket Dani drove, but she was still proceeding toward them.

"Stop her before she breaches the fence with all those rotters!" Evie exclaimed.

The car quickly turned down a side street restricting any shot from the two men and moments later a loud rumble of a revving engine could be heard over the moans of the dead that began shambling closer to the entrance.

"What's goin' on?" Del shouted as he sprinted across the street and up the barricade to join Evie and the two bikers.

"Dani's back and she brought a pack of rotters. I think she's going to try to bust through the fencing and kill us all," Evie shouted over the chaos.

The beater car reappeared jetting the opposite way up the street from which it had driven earlier, but for only a moment. Dani was gunning the car when she hit part of the fence that protected their little town full force. The chain link seemed to explode and disappear to each side as Dani burst through followed by a mob of the dead.

Rotters slowly filled the new entrance Dani had made dozens at a time. Evie, Jug, Swifty and Scoop scrambled down the barricade, each with a seemingly different plan and all began shouting as they ran in opposite directions. Evie started toward her house, she knew she would need to gather anything of value, like her lockbox of medications, but more importantly her baseball bat so that she might help fight. She felt almost certain the town would be lost.

"Tell everyone to meet at Hazel's. I'm getting the bus," Jug yelled.

A strong arm jerked Evie around and her uncle began pulling her in the other direction.

"I have to get the meds, Uncle Del! Grandma Birdie needs some of the pills I have. Let me go!" Evie exclaimed.

Del released her arm.

"We've got minutes before those things are all over this street. Meet me back at the giftshop and we're getting out of here," Del instructed.

Evie knew exactly what her uncle had in mind. They'd make their way back to his house and fly out.

"Okay, love you!" Evie shouted as she took off toward her residence and began running as quickly as her feet would take her.

Evie's lungs burned and she felt as though she might stumble she ran so hard and fast up the street. Others were coming out of their residences and Evie shouted for them to find the school bus and safety with Jug. Screams echoed from the next street over and Evie's thoughts quickly ran to Desmond, who lived just beyond the Health Department, near where the pandemonium concentrated.

She stopped, thinking she should check on him, but immediately she rationalized that with no weapon there would be very little she could accomplish. Once again her focus was on her house and she pushed herself even harder to get there as fast as she possibly could.

Up the side steps, quickly grabbing the bat from the inside door frame with one swift motion, Evie ran through the kitchen, bursting into the pantry and grabbed the lockbox of meds. She spun on her heels and ran back into the streets as quickly as she had entered the house. Her leg muscles burned as she dug her feet into the pavement pushing harder with each step in an effort to reach Desmond.

Jug now had the school bus pulled out into the street and people were piling into it. The town had become complete bedlam but Evie kept a cool head, dodging the others and quickly turned toward Desmond's house.

Shouts of warnings from other residents cautioned Evie that she was running straight for the epicenter of all the chaos, but she already knew that, and didn't care. She had to find Desmond.

As Evie turned the corner toward his house, she encountered not a few but dozens of the shambling rotters pouring into the streets and making their way toward the residents that were trying to escape. The herd seemed never-ending, men, women, children even elderly rotters all coming straight for her.

Evie tucked the heavy lockbox under her arm and grasped the bat with both hands as she ran toward Desmond's house. One zombie after another ran at her. Evie clinched up on the bat. Dropping the lockbox, she began swinging. The bat connected with the head of a female rotter and exploded. A spray of slimy sludge splattered across her face and hair and Evie wiped it away with her arm before she swung again at the next one. This one was a large man wearing a St. Louis Cardinals jersey. He looked a bit fresher so Evie swung harder and when the bat made contact, a tremendous jolt ran up her arm. The rotter fell to the ground, but Evie's hands stung.

Evie pushed her way toward Desmond's house, knocking one then another rotter to the ground as she gasped for breath.

"Desmond!" She shouted as she raced up his porch.

His front door was cracked open. Evie flung it wide and quickly scanned to room to find Desmond on the floor bleeding. Atop him was Dani holding a knife, looking as crazy as Evie had ever seen.

Dani glared at Evie, and the two girls lunged toward each other. Desmond, bloodied from an apparent knife wound to his shoulder, grabbed Dani's ankle and toppled the girl to the floor. Evie wasted no time and began pummeling Dani with the bat until her screams became moans.

"Evie! Behind you!" Desmond shouted.

He scrambled to his feet, pulling Evie behind him as rotters shuffled through the door, spilling into the living room.

One of the first flung itself at Desmond, but he pushed it back, knocking it to the ground next to where Dani lay. It took the creature only a mere few seconds to begin making a meal on the beaten girl, and several other zombies joined him.

Dani who had only been moaning from the beating she had received moments earlier from Evie now screamed with pure terror as the monsters took deep bites and tore into her flesh. The horror of it all made Evie pause, but Desmond pulled her from the gory scene and began dragging her through his house and out the back door.

"There's a box in the front I have to get!" Evie shouted.

Desmond seemed to pay her no mind but Evie pulled him in the direction of the discarded medication.

"We can't go back through there!" Des shouted.

"I need all those meds!" Evie screamed as she jerked away from his grasp and sprinted toward the front, baseball bat in hand, ready for the mob she knew would inevitably be there.

The box was just where she left it, yards away from Desmond's porch and Evie made haste in getting to it. Somehow she had managed to juke between and away from most of the rotters and she quickly grabbed the life saving prescriptions. Desmond grabbed Evie under the arm and began dragging her toward Hazel's.

"Jug has the bus ready to go outside of the diner," Evie spoke, realizing this would probably be the last time she would ever see Desmond.

"Okay, let's go!" Des smiled and began jogging in the direction of Hazel's.

"I'm not going. I have to get to my family," Evie responded, completely winded.

Desmond stopped.

"You don't want to go with me?" He asked, his tone not angry, but broken.

"I can't leave my family. Del wants to fly out of here," Evie explained.

"Then I'll make sure you get to them safe."

Evie's heart broke at the resolve Desmond seemed to have to help her find her family and do right by her. Hours ago she had agreed to marry the man, now she was leaving him. It all seemed wrong, but she couldn't leave her own family just to be with a guy she hardly knew. They needed her. They might not even be able to get to the runway without her. Uncle Del would have his hands full fighting off any rotters with the two women in tow. They weren't like her and her uncle. Retta and Birdie were kind, sweet and so not meant for a world like theirs had become.

Desmond's wound was bleeding, yet he fought and ran through the streets dragging Evie behind. She knew there was nothing she could do to help him at this point. They couldn't stop so she might take a look at the injury. Rotters had flooded town and Jug was now standing on top of the bus shouting for anyone to hurry up, that they'd be leaving soon.

Gunshots rang out in the direction of the giftshop and Desmond picked up his already hurried pace. The couple raced across the street to find a horde of rotters separating them from Evie's family and reaching for Evie's uncle. Del scaled the barricade and quickly dropped to the other side.

"They're leaving!" Desmond shouted in a panic.

He quickly pulled Evie back to the giftshop and slammed the door behind them.

"I'm sorry, Ev," Desmond bemoaned. "I'll figure out a way to get you to them."

Before Evie could respond, loud static startled her followed by a familiar voice.

"Evie, you there?" Delmont's voice boomed from the other room.

On the table Del used for reloading ammo, Desmond and Evie found one of the talkies the supply run guys used when they were in separate vehicles.

"I'm here!" Evie responded with a push of the button.

"Had to get your momma and granny to the car. I couldn't wait any longer."

"I'm sorry, Uncle Del, I can't get across the fence. There's too many!"

Desmond jerked the talkie out of Evie's hand.

"I'll get her to your place, Del. Get Birdie and Retta out of here, but don't leave until we get there. I promise, man, I won't let you down," Desmond said.

"Ten-Four," Del replied.

"The plane only holds four people," Evie explained.

"I know," Desmond answered.

"The bus is going to leave without you, you'll be stuck here alone!"

"I know. I don't care."

CHAPTER EIGHTEEN

The horn honked a few times and Evie heard the bus pull away. Desmond had officially sacrificed everything to make sure Evie found her way back to her family. The two were trapped inside the little giftshop. They took turns peering out the front and back windows to no avail. The rotter horde was only growing.

"Do we have some sort of plan?" Evie asked.

"Give me the box and just be ready to run," Desmond directed.

He peeped out the blinds of the front door once more and took a deep breath that was audible. Evie swallowed hard.

Desmond flicked the lock of the glass doors and slowly inched the door open. He slipped outside and motioned for Evie to follow.

A ratty hedgerow lined the building and Desmond pulled Evie behind it, crouching and slowly moving toward the edge of the building. When they ran out of shrubs, Desmond took her hand and nodded.

Without counting to three or taking a breath, the two were off and running as hard as they could through the sparse mob that now overtook what was left of Benton, Kentucky. The rotters were everywhere, but not as densely packed together as they were when they had flooded into town through the break in the fence Dani had made. Several feet separated most zombies and Desmond quickly navigated through the minefield of undead until they were surrounded by too many to avoid.

Desmond pushed one to the ground by slamming the lockbox into his chest, and Evie began beaning the heads of any within range. A hole within the mob presented itself and the two sidestepped through and ran the rest of the distance to Jug's welding shop and garage.

Fortunately Jug had left the door unlocked, but shut. Desmond knowing exactly where to find what he needed ran to the counter and pulled a set of keys from a row of nails holding several rings.

Evie followed him to the back of the garage where a row of motorcycles sat parked. Desmond began pushing one toward the front of the shop until it was resting up against the door they had just entered.

"You ready?" Desmond asked as he kicked one leg over the seat of the bike and sat.

"Don't you have helmets? I guess now would be a bad time to tell you I hate motorcycles?" Evie half-heartedly smiled.

"Just pretend you're my Old Lady and suck it up, Buttercup. You'll be fine," Des joked.

Evie carefully stretched her leg over the seat as well and situated herself behind him. Desmond handed her the box of medications and Evie nestled it between her legs and Desmond's back, and stretched her bat over the top. Holding both down with one hand, she slid the other around his waist.

Desmond started the motorcycle with a loud rumble and before Evie realized they were even going, Desmond burst through the cracked door and gunned the throttle. The bike vibrated and growled as they sped down the street and took a sharp turn toward Desmond's residence. Dodging rotters and obstacles at such a high rate of speed made Evie nervous, but she trusted Desmond, even when he sped toward the opening in the fence.

Evie squeezed her eyes shut, and tightened her grip around Desmond's waist. She took a deep breath and held it until she felt wind blowing through her hair and realized they were now on the open road.

***

Within a few minutes Evie would be reunited with her family. She was thrilled to be safely out of town, and also sickened at the idea of leaving Desmond. If only there was some way they could take him along, but there wasn't. The Mooney would hold no more than four people, and a night takeoff fully loaded would be precarious at best.

As the motorcycle turned into the gravel drive of Uncle Del's, Evie prepared herself for what she would need to do.

Desmond pulled past the drive and rode through the grass taking a straight line to the plane, which was already running and loaded. Birdie sat in the back and Retta and Del were in the front seats, Evie was sure eagerly anticipating her arrival. She looked to the end of the grass runway to find that her uncle had started what appeared to be some sort of fire to mark the end of the strip. He had everything ready to go and would waste no time.

When Desmond stopped, Evie hurdled herself off the motorcycle and ran toward the plane, medication in one hand and dropping her bat. She leaped onto the wing and leaned inside the plane, handing the box of meds to her grandmother.

"There's enough here for several months. Uncle Del, find her more. I love you all, but I've got to stay," Evie sobbed.

Retta hugged her daughter tight and began crying as well, "I won't ever see you again!"

Del reached to the back seat and pulled a radio from his flight bag. He handed it to Evie.

"My old Mooney is out on Airport Road. Ole boy I sold it to had it stored in one of the hangars there. I checked on it the other day during a run. Get out there and steal ya another plane, Hot Rod. I'm gonna fly south and try to land down at that little airport we used to fly to outside of Memphis. Meet you there," Del chuckled. "I had a feeling we'd need more than four seats if something happened."

"See you there!" Evie promised, and slammed the door shut.

She backed up but stopped close enough to still see her mother's face through the window as Del began his takeoff. The little plane rolled down the grass runway, and lifted off perfectly, just like she knew it would. Del was an awesome pilot.

With a huge grin on her face, Evie turned to find a dumbfounded Desmond standing behind her.

"You stayed behind for me?" He asked incredulously.

"Well, yes and no," Evie grinned. "I stayed behind to be with you, yes, but we aren't really staying behind. As it turns out, Del's old plane is still around and we're going to go get it and fly down to Tennessee and meet them," Evie excitedly beamed.

"I guess I probably should've mentioned before that I have an unnatural fear of flying, huh?"

"Just pretend you're *my* Old Lady and suck it up, Buttercup. You'll be fine."

ACKNOWLEDGEMENTS

It would be impossible to adequately thank everyone who has been so supportive in the creation of this book, but here goes...

First and foremost, I'd like to give my sincere appreciation and heartfelt gratitude to my great friend, Tim. Without your vast knowledge of all things that fly and incredible humor which kept me laughing throughout this learning process, this book would've never come to fruition. Thank you so much.

I'd also like to thank my mother, who listened to my storyline, offered some hilarious names for characters and is, and always will be my best friend and biggest supporter.

I don't just want, but need to thank my son, Ethan. Without you this book would've been completed years earlier, but life would've certainly been boring. I love you more than life, Goose.

Last, but certainly not least, I'd like to give a huge shout out and all my love to my readers. It humbles me each time a single book is sold. With so many options out there, thank you for buying my books, spending hours of your time to read them and especially to those who have reached out to let me know what they thought. I adore your feedback and messages. You guys rock.

ABOUT THE AUTHOR

T. MICHELLE NELSON IS AN AMERICAN AUTHOR OF PARANORMAL FICTION. SHE WAS BORN IN BENTON, KENTUCKY AND ATTENDED MURRAY STATE UNIVERSITY IN NEIGHBORING MURRAY, KENTUCKY. IN 2012 HER FIRST NOVEL *THE LIFE AND DEATH OF LILY DRAKE* WAS RELEASED. SINCE SHE HAS SUCCESSFULLY COMPLETED THE LILY DRAKE SERIES, WHICH CONSIST OF THREE BOOKS AND TWO SHORT STORIES. T. IS PRESENTLY WORKING ON HER NEW ZOMBIE SERIES AND CONTINUING TO PEN BOOKS ABOUT THE THINGS SHE LOVES TO WRITE ABOUT THE MOST - MONSTERS.

T. MICHELLE CURRENTLY RESIDES IN MOUNT VERNON, OHIO. WHEN SHE ISN'T WRITING, T. ENJOYS TRAVELING AND SPENDING TIME WITH HER FAMILY.

CPSIA information can be obtained at www.ICGtesting.com
Printed in the USA
LVOW11s1620111016

508320LV00003B/678/P